Serv

Vol. V

By Cassie Wild and M.S. Parker

ISBN-13:
978-1514381847

ISBN-10:
1514381842

Table of Contents

Chapter 1

Aleena

My heart was breaking and I felt sick inside.

Sick and furious. Sick for what had been done to the man I loved. Furious, in so many ways.

But none of that could matter right now.

This was going to be like the blind leading the blind, but as I leaned in, I knew that one of us would have to take the lead and it would have to be me. It didn't matter that he was older and more experienced in sex, or what roles we were supposed to have in the bedroom. I could only imagine what it had taken for Dominic to open up to me like that and I knew that I was going to have to take the next step.

"So here's the thing." My voice was husky and it hurt to even speak, but I made myself do it. If he could tell me all of that, I could tell him the full truth about what had happened between myself, Mitchell Pence and Penelope Rittenour. I owed him that. "The reason I left the party had nothing to do with Pence. He's a jerk, but I've dealt with worse."

Dominic's eyes flashed but when he went to speak, I touched my finger to his lips. "It's my turn to talk." I had to move my hand because the feel of his mouth was too distracting. "I left because of Penelope. She's a piece of work." I couldn't quite pull off the laugh. "She had me thinking you two..."

"We're not. We never——"

I nodded. "I'm getting that." Smoothing my hands up the solid length of his thighs, I leaned in and kissed his cheek. He tried to follow, but I moved away. "I was stupid. She got to me. I shouldn't have let her."

He fisted his hand in my hair and tried bring my mouth to his, need written across every line of his face.

Again, I pulled back until he released my hair. I needed him to hear this before things went any further.

"Relationships." I pressed my mouth to his once he'd eased up on my hair. It was a quicker kiss than I liked, but I couldn't lose myself before we'd finished the talk we should've had a while ago. "I get that you need to be in control and I understand it more than ever now. But, with relationships, it's a give and take. It can't just be about me having to trust you. You need to trust me too. Let me in. Can you do that?"

His eyes locked on mine, and I saw the struggle

on his face. Then, slowly, his hand fell away.

The ache in my heart deepened. The bruised look in his brilliant blue eyes was going to haunt me for a very long time. Right now, though, I was going to do my best to take it away.

"You said something earlier. Before we left." Leaning in, I tugged on his neck until he lowered his head and I could whisper in his ear. "Do you remember?"

He turned his face into my hair.

"Yes." The single word was ragged.

"Good."

I stood then and untied the belt to my robe. I rolled my shoulders, letting the heavy cotton fall to the floor. When I sank to my knees in front of him, I felt the slow glide of his gaze on me as if it was a caress.

Sliding my hands up his muscular chest, I dealt with his tie, his shirt. He helped strip them away, tossing them in a tangle somewhere off into the room.

When I went to tug at his pants, he rose and I sat back on my heels to watch him. Under the heavy fringe of his lashes, he watched back.

His blue eyes glowed, the fire in them oddly banked as he removed the rest of his clothes. I knew now, without having to know the details, where the marks on his body had come from; the ones I'd always just seen as part of who he was. I'd always thought him beautiful, and now, as I realized all the scars he hid inside, he seemed even *more* beautiful.

He stood there in front of me and I placed my

hands on his thighs, skimmed them up, felt the light growth of his hair tickling my palms as I stroked up, then down, then up.

His erection pulsed, beating in time with the blood flooding his veins. The thick shaft stiffened, rose, another beautiful part of his body. The vein that ran along the underside of his cock caught my eye as I sat back on my heels. I flicked a look up at him before I leaned forward.

Slowly, I rose up. His eyes remained locked on me as I closed my mouth around the swollen head. A harsh noise ripped out of him and he lifted a hand. It hovered at his side for a second and then, without saying a word, he lowered it.

"Will you lie on the bed?" I asked, my voice a low whisper.

It was quiet. I was almost afraid to speak, afraid to shatter the odd spell that had fallen between us.

His gaze never left my face as he slowly sat down, then pushed himself back on the bed. He didn't lie down though, but propped himself up on his elbows, watching me as I stood, then climbed onto the bed, moving between his legs.

Was it hard, I wondered, for him to do this?

As the thought came to me, I caught sight of the muscle throbbing in his jaw and knew the answer. It *was* hard for him.

Yielding control, even for something as simple as this, would be almost impossible. I put my hand on his thigh again and felt the muscles tense and tighten under his skin. I wrapped my free hand around his cock and stroked up, then down.

4

A groan rumbled out of him.

I did it again, then leaned down to swirl my tongue across the head. I sucked gently, rolling my eyes up to look at him as I increased the suction. He swore and thrust his hips up, shoving his cock deeper into my mouth. My eyes started to water and I pulled up.

He made a move as if to grab me, but again, he stopped and swore, falling back flat on the bed this time and flinging an arm over his eyes.

One hand curled into a tight, desperate fist. His jaw clenched and his cheekbones jutted out against his skin. And when I took him back into my mouth, he made that same raw sound, followed by my name as he rocked up to me.

I did it again and again.

The world shrank down to us, that bed and the rhythm of his hips as he rose to meet my mouth as I sucked on him.

Need burned and twisted inside me but I ignored it.

I needed this more—and he needed *me*.

I could feel it in the restrained way he didn't *let* himself reach for me, in the desperate way he didn't let himself take over.

He growled my name and fisted his hands in the thick comforter, twisting at the material as he started to pump his hips in hard, rapid circles. My mouth ached, my lips stretched tight around his width, but I took as much as I could. He started to come, the taste of him salty on my tongue. My eyes watered and I needed air, but I didn't let myself pull away, determined to swallow it all.

Not until the tension left his body and not until I had milked the last drop of semen from his cock, only then did I lift my head. His eyes were on me, dark and burning, his face so full of emotion that I could barely breathe.

I crawled up onto the bed and curled up next to him. He immediately pulled me up against him, his arms wrapping around me and holding me close. His hand threaded through my hair and then trailed down my bare shoulder. "Aleena..."

"Hmmm?"

He didn't say anything else.

Just my name.

Closing my eyes, I snuggled closer and closed my eyes. "I have to tell you something," I said softly. "I..."

I licked my lips, tasting him again. I was terrified to say the words that were trapped inside me, but I had to. I couldn't keep them locked up anymore and I was dying, bit by bit, day by day, living like this. I couldn't tell him that we needed to trust each other if I wasn't being honest.

Slowly, I lifted my head and looked at him.

His lashes lifted and I could see the shield ready to slam back into place.

I touched his cheek. "I..."

Just do it. Do it and be done.

"I love you." I tried to smile and failed. "I didn't mean for it to happen and I don't expect anything from you." I looked away. "But I can't pretend anymore and whatever we're doing, how we're doing it...Dominic, it's killing me. I either..."

I sat up. His arms fell away and I felt terribly cold, suddenly all too aware that I was naked. Staring towards the window, I blinked away the tears.

"I can't be the kind of woman Penelope is, or the kind of woman your mother is. I don't want to be some pretty little piece you tuck up in your room." Hollow, I drew my legs up, trying to get some warmth. "I...look, I understand that relationships aren't easy for you and I can...I understand and I don't want to push you on anything. But if you...I just..."

Now I felt pissed off and angry with myself. I should have just let it go. I made a move to shove off the bed.

Dominic caught my wrist and tugged me back, pulling me on top of him. I caught my breath, ready to have him roll us and pin me under him. To put himself back in control.

But he didn't. He held me.

"You just what?" he asked, his voice calm.

Through my tears, I stared at him.

"You just *what*?" he asked again.

I blinked, uncertain of what I'd meant to say or what I'd even been thinking.

"I told you, Aleena," he said, his voice patient. "I don't know how to do this, so if you want something, you have to tell me."

"I want you." My voice broke and I was furious with myself for it. "But if I can't have *all* of you, then I'd rather we..."

7

His mouth caught mine.

Now he rolled and pinned me under him.

He was naked and hot and smooth and I gasped as he pressed against me, hard again. "All of me," he said against my lips. "You'll have all of me, Aleena. And you better be ready for it, because dammit, I'll have all of you, too."

He braced his hands on the bed next to my shoulders and stared down at me. I gasped as he thrust, deep and hard and high.

"Take me," he said, watching me. "All of me."

I clung to him. "All of you..."

As though he'd just been waiting to hear my affirmation, he started to move quicker, harder, faster. There was no finesse, no games, only heat and friction and pleasure. He drove into me hard enough that it should've hurt, but I only wanted him to go deeper. He didn't tease, but I still begged, the need I had for him twisting with the fire inside me until I exploded. He swore as my pussy tightened around his cock but didn't stop. Over and over he slammed into me, pushing me higher and higher until he came again, calling my name.

We clung to each other even as we came down, our need not merely a sexual one. We needed each other in ways I wasn't quite sure I fully understood yet. But it didn't matter. We had time.

I fell asleep smiling, my body still entwined with his.

Chapter 2

Aleena

A camera flashed in my eyes and I blinked away the spots.

Dominic guided me away from it and I instinctively followed.

A couple of weeks ago, I'd *wanted* this, I reminded myself. And, okay, it had been nice to have Dominic call from the office while I was working at home and ask if he could take me out to dinner.

It had been nice indeed.

No, I admitted, it had been *more* than nice.

The entire past week had been great. Even with people shoving cameras into my face, I wouldn't have traded it. It happened whenever Dominic and I went out, twice without him even around. Fortunately, his drivers knew how to handle things and had been able to get me away without too much trouble.

Tonight, though, he *was* around and more than a few seemed to think there was blood in the water.

That was a shark thing, right? And the media was very shark-like. They moved after people in a herd, attacked together though each one was desperate for their own pound of flesh. They thinned out the weakest and then focused on those left standing after the melee.

It was an unsettling and disconcerting sensation, one I didn't like at all.

"Ms. Davison! Ms. Davison! Is it true your mother broke up a happy relationship back in Iowa?"

That voice rang out from the crowd and I came to a stunned stop. Surprised, I turned my head, trying to find the one who'd asked the question. While I'd been photographed and speculated about, this was the first time someone had singled me out for a question that wasn't just about my relationship with one of the city's most eligible bachelors.

Dominic tugged on my hand. "Come on, Aleena. Don't give them what they want," he said, bending his head to murmur in my ear.

Holding his blue eyes with mine, I took a deep breath and nodded. I let him lead me to the curb where the car waited, door already open. Maxwell gave each of us a nod as we ducked inside, into blissful, sweet silence.

"Where did they come from?" I asked, looking out the tinted window. "And how did they get my name?"

"Barracudas can find anything, baby," Dominic answered irritably. Then he shot me a look that said he knew how he'd sounded. "I'm sorry. I wanted to

10

have a nice evening with you."

"It was nice." Leaning against him, I stared out at the city as it drifted by in a slow sprawl of lights and motion. I loved New York. I loved it more all the time. Barracudas notwithstanding. "Maybe some camera-welding fiends interrupted it, but I still had fun."

Dominic curled his arm around me and brought me in closer. I snuggled in against his strong body, feeling the muscles firm beneath his shirt. His fingers trailed along the low neckline of my dress and I shivered. My nipples hardened against the silk and lace of my bra. When he pressed his lips against my temple, warmth raced through me.

"The night's not over yet." The words held the promise of pleasure...and pain.

"No." Heat slid through me in a slow, easy glide. "It's not."

***

"You can't speak."

Dominic brought the flogger down on my ass.

I bit my lip to hold in the words as the sting spread across my skin, joining with the heat already there. I'd once fallen asleep outside while sunbathing on my stomach and when I'd woken up, I'd been burnt. It had been the only sunburn I'd ever had—with skin like mine, it took a lot more to burn—but I remembered that feeling now. My ass

11

felt like it was on fire.

"You want to speak, don't you?"

I jerked my head in a nod, taking a short, gasping breath. He brought the flogger down again and a new burst of painful pleasure went through me. My head fell back and I curled my hands into fists, my nails biting into the skin of my palms.

"Spread your legs."

I didn't. I was afraid to. He wasn't using the softer cat that he'd used before, so even though he wasn't hitting me hard, the pain was more intense.

"Spread your legs, Aleena." There was a bit of coaxing to his command, but I still resisted and this time, instead of speaking, he used the handle of the flogger and nudged it between my thighs. It rubbed between my legs, back and forth, back and forth. There was a hint of teasing laughter in his voice as he said, "I could make you come like this. Should I?"

I didn't know what I wanted. To come. To end this torture. To let him take me to new heights in ways I didn't understand. I did know one thing though. He'd told me not to talk. I bit down on my inner cheek hard enough to taste blood and he rewarded me by twisting the handle of the crop, scraping it against my clitoris. I gasped, jerking against my restraints.

My wrists were bound. He'd used velvet ropes, and they had felt soft against my skin at first, but now, the material cut into my skin with a delicious bite. The velvet was looped through the metal circle at the top of the pole, high enough that my arms were stretched out, but low enough that I was able to stay flat-footed, even when bent at a slight angle.

He rubbed the handle against me again. Then again. I shuddered and tried to twist away. The sensation was too much. Intense and erotic. Clamping my legs together didn't do much good though. It only served to trap the handle of the flogger between my thighs and when he twisted this time, I felt every exquisite nuance. Something very much like a strangled moan fell from my lips.

He sighed and I could almost hear his amusement. "You're going to be difficult tonight, aren't you?"

"No," I gasped out the word, and the very second I did, I knew I'd messed up.

A finger trailed down my spine and I knew Dominic was smiling. I could feel it.

He turned me to face him. "I was hoping you'd disobey at some point tonight," he said, his tone soft, as though he was confiding something.

I shivered when he ran his hands down along my ribcage, his thumbs caressing the sides of my breasts.

"Because you see, there's something I want to do. Something I've been wanting for a while." He pressed the handle against me again, harder this time, moving it in a deliberate fashion that had me rocking against him, against the firm, rounded, ridged grip that felt entirely too good.

I could feel the orgasm building inside. So close. Just a little bit more and—

He stopped.

I sucked in a breath and lifted my head, glaring

at him as he strode across the room.

"From the first moment I saw, I've had this image in my head," he said over his shoulder. He paused and looked at me, as if waiting for me to ask.

No way in hell. I pressed my lips more tightly together. He chuckled and I knew he'd seen the answer in my eyes. I was a mass of writhing nerves, anxiety and anticipation mixed into one. But I wasn't going to break the rules again, not when I knew he was going to tell me anyway.

Struggling to regulate my breathing, I watched as he opened the closet and reached inside. He pulled out something long and slim. It sort of looked like a curtain rod except there were loops on the end. When he met my eyes, he smiled and lifted one of the loops...no, not a loop exactly. It was a cuff.

"This is a spreader bar," he said softly. "It does exactly what it sounds like."

Oh shit.

My breathing started to hitch as he knelt between my thighs. I could feel his hot breath on my skin as he leaned down and grasped my ankle. First the right, his fingers lingering on my calf as he finished. His touch became firm as he moved my legs further apart, then fastened the second cuff around my left ankle. He caressed my calf for a moment, then sat back on his heels.

"Now you're completely open to me," Dominic said. The satisfaction in his voice sent heat rushing through me.

Heat and a tinge of embarrassment and all sorts of vulnerability. The stance was slightly uncomfortable, but I barely noticed because I was all too aware of how visible everything was now.

I jerked as he ran his fingertip between my lips.

"And so wet." He looked at me as he stood, sliding his finger into his mouth.

That shouldn't be so hot.

He turned me back around, the ropes untwisting as I went. It was awkward, trying to move with my legs spread like that, but I managed, shivering as cool air moved over my wet, sensitive skin. Once I was in place, he slid the flogger up between my thighs and I felt each of the tassels. It made me shiver. It made me quake.

And then I cried out as he brought it down on my ass.

A moment later, a softer blow followed, but not on my ass. This one was straight between my thighs on my exposed pussy.

Whimpering, I jerked against the restraints.

Dominic said, "You came once before with the other cat. Do you think I could bring you to climax with this one as well?"

I was panting, unable to answer even if I'd thought he wanted one.

Another lash on my bottom.

Then the backs of my thighs.

Then *between* my legs.

A river of heat lit up from that delicious, tormenting blow. Pain and fire and pleasure and so many overwhelming sensations that I couldn't even begin to describe.

One blow to my butt.

Thighs.

Between.

Again.

Again.

I started to shake, feeling the climax building inside me. I found myself pushing back towards him, wanting, needing...

And then he stopped.

I tensed, my breath locked in my lungs—was he...a test. He was testing me. Toying with me. A test of trust. My trust in him that he'd make this good for me.

Something landed on the bed in front of me, brushing against my thigh as it went by. I looked down and stared, dazed, at the flogger that lay on the mattress. Dammit! Frustrated need twisted in my gut, a fist there.

"Please," I whispered.

He turned me around more easily than before by simply lifting me off the floor. No need to walk. Gentle hands cupped my face, lifted my lips for a kiss. His mouth was soft against mine, a surprising contrast to his prior ministrations. My body throbbed with need. The need to feel him, to feel the flogger, to feel those lashes between my thighs...something. Anything that would relieve the pressure inside me.

I felt a tug at my wrists as he broke the kiss. As he lowered my arms, I couldn't suppress the groan of relief. Pins and needles rushed through my veins. He reached around me and when he straightened, I saw a bottle of lotion in his hand. He opened it and I

16

smelled vanilla. Without a word, he massaged the cool liquid into my chafed skin. The sharp need inside me softened and spread. With just this gesture, he reminded me that I could trust him, not only for my pleasure, but to take care of me as well.

When he was finished, he tossed the bottle back where he'd gotten it, and shifted me so that I was standing a few feet further from the bed.

"What are you...?"

"Quiet." It was a command, no matter how softly spoken.

I nodded my understanding. He helped me down onto my knees, then pressed on my back. I leaned forward until I was resting on my elbows. He still had the spreader bar in place and I caught my breath when I realized just what other purpose it served. I was face down on the floor, my butt high in the air, every part of me spread apart and ready for the taking.

Before I could even think, he was inside me and I screamed at the fullness of his invasion. Too much, too fast. He withdrew and surged back inside, bringing another raw, rough noise to my lips. I was wet, but not stretched and he was big, rubbing against every inch of me.

He brought his hand down hard on my ass and then—

I froze, every muscle in my body instantly tense. Waiting. Afraid. Not afraid.

He cursed as my pussy tightened around him, but he pressed his thumb against my asshole again. I twisted away, or tried to, but I was caught. He fisted his free hand in my hair and tugged me up, holding me in place. My palms were flat on the floor, taking most of my weight, but pain still radiated down from my scalp. Between the spreader bar, being impaled on his cock and the grip he had on my hair, I couldn't move.

"I want you to be still for me now, Aleena," he said, his voice even, as if he wasn't buried balls deep inside me. "Do you understand me?"

"Yes, sir." I couldn't breathe.

He pressed harder and I could feel my muscles working to keep him out. "Do you remember the word you use if you want me to stop?"

I tried to nod, but couldn't. The grip he had on my hair was too tight. Forcing the words out through my tight throat, I said, "Yes. I remember."

"If you use it, I'll stop and we'll be done. But if you don't..." He made a strange little twisting movement with his thumb, the tip of it popping past the ring of muscle.

I cried out, falling forward as he released my hair. Scrabbling at the floor, I tried again to pull away and I opened my mouth, ready to say it, ready to say the word that would make him stop.

"Does it hurt?" Dominic asked. His voice was calm, but I could hear the undercurrent of emotion in the question. Concern, but also desire. Need. Need not only to do this for his pleasure, but for mine. Need for me to trust him. "Aleena..."

I wanted to say yes. Yes, it hurt. But...it didn't.

I could feel the top part of his thumb inside my ass, less than an inch, and it didn't feel *good*,

18

exactly. It was strange and tight and too intimate. Embarrassing and odd. But...it didn't really hurt.

Closing my eyes, I forced myself to answer. "No."

He pulled his thumb out.

I breathed out a sigh of relief and focused on the rhythm of his hips. Slow swivels and shallow, lazy strokes that relaxed my body.

Too lazy, I realized a few moments later, as his hand returned to the narrow opening between my cheeks and his fingers were wet and slick. I could smell cinnamon mixing with the vanilla lotion on my wrists.

"I've got lubricant on my fingers," he said as he rubbed them against my anus. "I'm going to touch you again and put my finger inside your ass. All the way this time."

I shuddered. "Dominic...no. I don't..." Panic fluttered in my stomach.

"Remember how you make me stop."

I arched up in shock as he started to push his finger inside. It was too small and it burned, my muscles fighting against the intrusion. I cried out as he kept going, forcing my ass to open wide to accept his whole finger. Then he was in and I whimpered, my entire body trembling.

"Relax," Dominic said. "You're fighting me."

No shit! I would have shouted it, except I was still having trouble breathing. My chest felt tight. My skin felt tight. Constricted. Then he started to move his finger inside me, slow, careful thrusts. As his hips began to move, he matched each stroke, neither one hurried or rough, but filling me more completely than I knew was possible. Before I realized it, the strange, peculiar sensations gave away to a pleasure that was almost more than I could handle. I gasped as something tight inside me relaxed.

Distantly, I heard Dominic murmur, "That's it...take it, baby. Take it..."

I don't know what he was talking about, but I found myself rocking back against him. Riding his cock. Riding his hand.

"I'm going to give you more," he told me.

I swore as a second finger worked its way into me. The burn and pain was back, but it mixed with the pleasure more quickly this time. His cock moved faster and the hand on my hip tightened until I knew I was going to have bruises. Then he twisted his fingers and I cried out.

He drove into me.

Harder.

Faster.

I pushed back to meet his every thrust, the need for him, for release, overriding any embarrassment I might have felt otherwise. He stopped moving the fingers in my ass, keeping them buried inside me as he pounded into me. And then I was coming, my arms shaking so badly that I couldn't hold myself up, but then I didn't have to because his hand was in my hair again, twisting my head around so he could kiss me. I bit his bottom lip and he came.

It was hard and it was messy and I almost blacked out as he rode me from one orgasm into another.

***

We were curled up on the couch later when Dominic slid a hand down and cupped my ass. I hissed as my skin stung under his touch. He'd used the same vanilla lotion on every place he'd used the flogger and it soothed some of the burning, but I was still sensitive.

"Did you enjoy it?" The question sounded casual, but I could feel the tension in his body.

Immediately, blood rushed to my face as I thought about what we'd done. "Wasn't that obvious?"

I stared hard at the TV. We'd spent several evenings together lately. We'd gone out. We'd gone to the movies. We'd made love in the kitchen on the floor while the food I'd been cooking burned. And we'd cuddled on the couch, content to just be with each other.

It was as close to bliss as I'd ever been and I thought maybe, just maybe, things could work out. But I still didn't know how to handle all these crazy, embarrassing questions he liked to ask. How was I supposed to say that I'd enjoyed the pain of the flogger? That I'd enjoyed having his fingers in my ass while he fucked me? Where I came from, those weren't things good girls were supposed to like. I might've grown up a lot since coming here, but I still thought of myself as a good girl.

He turned his face into my hair and I shivered as he sought out my ear and nipped it, just hard

21

enough to hurt.

"Answer the question."

I had to swallow, then clear my throat—twice—before I could. "I'm not sure." I did know I couldn't answer while I was touching him.

Wiggling away, I sat on the edge of the couch and then flicked him a look. His gaze rested on me, his blue eyes steady. He always looked so unaffected while I felt like *everything* in me was in distress. I understood his need to be in control, but I sometimes wished that I could know for certain that I had some sort of effect on him.

"I...well, it felt good." My cheeks blazed even hotter. I forced myself to be completely honest. I understood that my role as Sub was not only to obey, but to make sure he knew how I felt. "It did hurt. A little. Then it felt really good." I made myself meet his eyes. "But I'm getting the feeling you want to put something a lot bigger than your finger in my ass."

"Yes," he said. "I do." He held out a hand.

Slowly, I put mine in his and he gave me a reassuring squeeze. When he tugged, I went to him, kneeling at his side so that I could face him more easily. I knew if he wanted me to move, he'd let me know.

He ran his fingers through my hair, rubbed his thumb over my lips. The mask he wore so often was slipping away and I could see the real him beneath. His voice was rough. "I want to have every part of you. I want to know every part of you."

His thumb pressed against my lips and I opened my mouth, darting my tongue out to lick the pad of his thumb. He made a sound low in his throat and I knew I was getting what I wanted. He was showing me, telling me, how much I affected him.

His hand slid down my neck, fingers wrapping around my throat. Not squeezing, just there, the simple weight of them a reminder of his strength. "I want to feel my cock in your throat and I want to feel you come against my mouth. I want to feel your nails tearing the skin of my back and I want to hear you sobbing my name as I fill every part of you with my cock." He bent forward, his body surrounding mine. I shivered as he slid a hand down my back and palmed my ass. "I want you to mark me with your teeth and mouth." He nipped at the side of my neck. "And I want to leave my mark on you so everyone knows that you're mine."

I closed my eyes. Fuck. He pulled back enough so that he could raise my face to look at him. I didn't need the command to open my eyes. His eyes were blazing as he continued, burning with desire so strong I didn't know if I could stand it.

"I want to fill every last part of you. I want to see you shaking as you fight to take me. And I want to see your eyes widen as the pain gives way to pleasure and I want to feel you break for me when you finally come."

I was practically panting by the time he finished.

"So," I asked weakly. "When do we start?"

Chapter 3

Dominic

When do we start?

She'd asked me that question more than fourteen hours ago and although logically I knew it wasn't the case, I still felt like I was still sporting the hardest damn erection in the history of the world.

I could have been a real bastard and taken her right then.

It didn't matter that she was untried for what I wanted from her. I could have made her ready and I could have made her want it.

Fuck that.

She already wanted it.

I could have made her beg for it.

But I wanted her ready. Really ready so that there were no doubts, no second-guessing and no regrets. More than that, I wanted to do the right thing for her.

Still, I would have her yielding everything to me when the time came.

I'd have her bound and bent over, vulnerable and begging.

And I'd fill her so slowly, she'd be squirming and sobbing before I even pushed my head through that tight ring of muscles.

Then I'd have her twisting and writhing around me, coming from my cock in her ass.

But not yet.

Definitely not right now.

Brooding, I stared at the name that flashed up on my agenda and then moved to the door, sincerely hoping that my thoughts weren't making themselves known on my body.

Aleena and Amber were talking quietly as they went over some of the information for the interviews they had lined up this week. One of the interviews was a woman from *Devoted*. Joely had worked for the match making company for nearly a decade, and both Aleena and Amber had come to the same conclusion as I had. Joely was underutilized, underpaid, and she either needed to transfer out or find a job where she could put her skill-set to use.

I personally preferred to keep the talent for myself, so she was on the schedule for an interview later in the day. She wasn't my current appointment, however, and she definitely wasn't the reason I was pissed off.

So far, the little shit was five minutes late. That didn't bode well for him. Not that this would be pleasant for him to begin with.

"Aleena." She looked up and I had to force myself to keep my voice professional. Every time I

26

looked at her, desire hit me hard. I couldn't show it here though. "When he gets here, I want you to bring him back."

Aleena's eyes flashed, but her voice was polite. "Sir?"

Shit. "Hear me out." I put my hands in my pockets to keep from making a gesture of surrender. I'd put her in a terrible place without realizing it, but I had to maintain my position in front of Amber. What I really wanted to do was take the man who'd insulted her—who'd put his fucking hands on her—and break every bone in said hands. But I had to be a businessman first, play it smart.

First.

And once he fucked up again?

I'd rip his balls off and have them for breakfast.

"Bring him back," I said again as she crossed her arms over her chest in a gesture I recognized all too well. She drew her head back, a haughty look on her face. That look made me want to bite her. It made me want to pull up her skirt and bury my cock inside her. Take her hard and fast until she was screaming my name.

She must have seen something of what I felt because her chest rose sharply and the pupils in her eyes dilated. She shifted her weight from one foot to the other and I wondered if her panties were wet.

Fuck.

If we'd been alone...

But we weren't.

"I sent him a standard contract last night." I studied her face as I explained and saw

27

understanding immediately dawn in her eyes. Those contracts contained standard clauses on sexual harassment and issues on gender and racial equality, among other matters. "I received confirmation of its delivery, so I'll ask him if he did, and naturally, I'll ask him if he read it. I'm going to have him sign off. Then..." I blew out a breath and tucked my hands into my pockets. "I'm transferring him here. I want him out, but I can't keep an eye on him when he's in Philly and I'm here."

"You want me to be, what, bait?"

I could tell by the look on her face exactly what she thought of that, but she at least looked like she was going to let me explain.

"No. Not bait. I'm not setting him up or trying to catch him. I couldn't legally do that." My smile was small and tight. "But he's going to act how he's going to act. I'd prefer him to do it in a place where nobody will make allowances for him and cover for him. And where I could take swift and immediate action."

Aleena considered this for a moment and then gave a curt nod. "All right. But if he touches me one more time, I might just break his hand."

That wouldn't be an issue. If Mitchell Pence touched her one more time, he might not have any hands left to break. I hated men like him to begin with, ones who thought their position and power meant they could touch anyone they wanted, do whatever they wanted, no matter whom they hurt. I would've fired him no matter who'd been on the receiving end. That it had been Aleena just made it more personal.

Before she could move away, I tucked a piece of hair behind her ear. She'd started wearing it down when she worked and, while I loved how it looked, I found it terribly distracting, remembering what it looked like spread on my pillow. "Thank you," I said quietly. "For understanding."

When she looked back up at me, she was smiling. It wasn't her usual bright, wide smile, but it was genuine.

I started to move closer, but suddenly realized that Amber was still in the room. I looked up, but she was already heading for the door.

"Smoke break," she called over her shoulder.

I was pretty sure she was grinning, but I didn't really care at the moment. I closed the distance between Aleena and I until we were closer than was workplace appropriate—but I didn't touch her. I knew if I did, I couldn't guarantee I'd be able to control myself. And with Mitchell Pence overdue, being caught kissing Aleena wouldn't be good. I could, however, say one of the things that had been on my mind all morning.

"You were already up and in the shower when I woke up. I'd thought about joining you in your bed."

A shiver ran through her.

With the exception of occasionally passing out for an hour or two after sex, we still didn't sleep together. Either she went to her bed or we both went our separate ways, depending on where we'd had sex. She never asked to stay and I never told her I wanted her to. I wasn't sure if I did, or even if she wanted to sleep in the same bed. And I had absolutely no clue how to broach the subject, even if I decided I wanted to.

But I did know that there was nothing quite so pleasurable as crawling into bed with Aleena in the morning and waking her up degree by slow degree—or perhaps I should say, inch by slow inch—when I came inside her and watched her wake up as she took me in. Or when I took advantage of her not being in her submissive role and woke her by bringing her to orgasm with my mouth and fingers before sliding into that tight, wet heat...

Her lips parted as if she was going to say something, but the elevator made a faint chime, interrupting.

We both stepped away. I took a shuddering breath as I moved into my office. Just before I closed the door, she slid me a look.

It was heated and full of promise.

Fuck. How was I supposed to concentrate when she was looking at me like that?

Closing the door, I strode to my desk, forcing myself to focus on the asshole I had to talk to. I pushed a button as I sat down and looked at the security feed going into my computer, including the monitor in the outer office, where Mitchell Pence was moving toward Aleena with a predatory look in his eyes.

I'd intended to stay quiet and let Aleena bring him in rather than me going out to get him, but I was flexible. Depressing the intercom, I kept my eyes on his face as I barked, "Aleena, has my ten-thirty shown up yet? This tardiness is unacceptable."

Pence jerked to a stop and he spun away from Aleena. He made a slashing motion at her, drawing a hand across his throat. I knew what he meant, but there was still an air of menace to it that made my hands curl into fists. I wanted nothing more than the opportunity to hear his sniveling nose crunching under my knuckles.

"One moment, sir," Aleena's voice said through the intercom. She sounded calm and cool, but I could see the tension on the monitor.

Take your time. I hit the control that allowed me to hear the conversations out in the office. We didn't have sound everywhere, but in my waiting room, I did. Amber had made sure of it since she was usually the one out there. Aleena only filled in when Amber wasn't available. Like now.

Pence hissed, "Tell him my driver was late. A wreck in front of my hotel. Unavoidable. I called and left a message."

"I don't have a message, Mr. Pence."

His eyes narrowed. "You will tell him I left a message. I don't give a fuck if you have it or not."

I couldn't see Aleena's face, but I didn't need to. I heard the reproach in her voice. "Perhaps you should give him the message, Mr. Pence. I'll let him know you're here." Before he could say anything else, Aleena hit the button. "Mr. Snow? Your appointment is here. He wanted me to tell you about a wreck. In front of his hotel."

I grunted. "Bring him back, please. Thank you." Instead of shutting down the security feed, I split the screen and brought up the news. He'd asked for a room at the Waldorf. A wreck there may or may not make the news, depending on how big of a wreck it was, but hey, I could at least pretend to look.

Aleena opened the door. Pence stood a little too close behind her. Aleena quickly stepped out of his way, but he still managed to brush into her as he came inside. "Thanks, sugar," he said, his voice jovial.

"Ms. Davison."

She arched a brow. "Yes, Mr. Snow?"

I shook my head at her and then glared at Mitchell Pence.

He came striding toward me, hand outstretched. Roughly five feet away, he realized something was wrong and he slowed. "Good morning, Dominic."

It took all my control to keep my tone even halfway civil. "Her name, Mitchell, is *Ms*. Davison. Not sugar. Not sweetheart. Not honey. Not even Aleena. You will call her Ms. Davison. Period."

Slowly, the smile faded from his face and he lowered his hand to his side. He glanced over at Aleena and then back at me. He tried for the kind of smile that I'd seen men like him give when they were caught. "Look, Dominic. I think I know where this is coming from. I know I had a few too many last week and I'd be happy to apologize—"

"Good." I sat down behind my desk and gestured toward Aleena, letting her know she could go. "I'll have her work email address forwarded on to you. A formal letter of apology for your sexist, racist remarks would go a long way in convincing me that you understand my obvious concerns. Please be sure to copy the email to me so I can make sure it gets into your file." I gave him a thin smile. "It will smooth things over on your transfer here."

Pence gaped at me.

"Now, let's discuss your job des—"

The shock subsided and he leaned forwarded, hands braced on my desk. "Wait a minute."

Head cocked, I asked, "I'm sorry. Was I unclear? I can have Amber come in to dictate and send the notes to your email, if you wish."

"I don't want anybody *dictating* something to me." He bit off each word, his eyes narrow. He had the sort of tan that came from a tanning bed, artificial and almost painstakingly perfect. There were faint, pale lines around his eyes from where the protective lenses sat when he lay on the bed. I wondered if he'd had a hair transplant too. I seemed to remember him having a slight bald spot in one of the company's pictures.

Hands braced on the desk, he leaned in. "Are you really expecting me to write that girl a fucking letter? Because I responded when she flirted with me?"

So that's how you're going to play it. Pushing back from the desk, I folded my hands on my lap and said, "That is how a formal apology usually goes. You write a letter. The one you offended reads it. It's done."

"Look, Snow—"

"*Mr.* Snow." I snapped back and pointed at a seat. When he went to snarl, I held up a hand. He sat down. "Before we get off track, I assume you received the information I sent you last night?"

He made a dismissive gesture. "Yeah. What of it?"

"You read it?"

Pence crossed his arms, looking more like a petulant child than a grown man. "Sure."

"Good. Then you'll know sexism, racism, anything that demeans any human being because of their race, sex, class, sexual preference...none of that is tolerated here, and is grounds for immediate termination, regardless of any deals or contracts." I gave him a moment for that to sink in. "Since you and Aleena started off on the wrong foot, it will be best to smooth things out so your transfer here goes smoothly." I paused and then smiled at him. "You *do* want it to go smoothly, I assume. Unless you want to return and work under Miriam Beckham?"

A vein pulsed in his temple. "I want to be where the action is, Mr. Snow."

"Then let's get to work."

I gave him a week.

***

He didn't make it two hours.

Aleena had one hand on my arm, as if to hold me back, although it wasn't necessary. I was done.

Mitchell Pence was on the floor, gagging, curled

34

up in the fetal position and cradling his balls.

You must suck cock really well. You've got Snow twisted—

I'd heard that much come out of his mouth before Aleena had shoved him back and told him to get away from her. If she'd looked at me the way she'd been looking at him, I'd have been running for the door.

Not him. He'd grabbed her arm and I'd seen red.

My brain had somehow managed to function even when some primal part of me had been processing along the basest level, because while I was imagining ripping his dick off and choking him with it, I'd heard myself calmly telling him to gather his things. Security would escort him out.

He'd pushed me. Not physically, but with a few remarks I'd assumed he'd thought were sly and clever.

I'd just smiled at him and pushed back, mentioned a few things I'd heard here and there regarding his sexual prowess...or lack thereof.

He'd hit me and I'd laughed, saying that must've meant the rumors were true.

He'd hit me again and that was when I'd let myself drive my fist into his mouth. Blood spurted and I was pretty sure I felt a few teeth crack. Even as he reeled back, I'd caught his tie and stopped him, jerked him close and did my best to shove my knee into his chest cavity via his groin. I didn't usually hit below the belt. Most men wouldn't. After what Aleena had told me about her conversation with Miriam Beckman's husband regarding Mitchell, I

35

figured Pence deserved it.

He was still twitching and shuddering, making odd little noises.

"Come on," I said. "Get up."

His eyes wheeled toward me and he scrabbled at the floor. I wanted to kick him until he begged me to stop. Make him apologize to Aleena and every other woman he'd ever put his slimy little hands on. I wanted to beat the shit out of him for ever thinking he could force his attentions on someone who didn't want them...

"Dominic, love," Aleena said softly. "It's enough."

Her voice pulled me back and when I looked down at her, I realized my hands were shaking. She squeezed my arm as the doors to the elevators slid open and security stepped out. I watched Amber and Aleena share a look as Aleena dropped her hand. She didn't move away from me though. Amber stepped towards the security guards as Aleena spoke.

"Let's get you cleaned up, Mr. Snow."

Her words didn't make any sense until I felt her guiding me back towards my office. I went with her, trying to tie down the adrenaline still coursing through my veins. Once inside, she shut the door and went to my private bathroom. A few moments later, she came out with a wet paper towel and reached for my hand. She began to wipe the blood from my bruised knuckles, the touch of her skin burning my already overheated flesh.

I needed.

I reached for her and she made no move to stop me as I picked her up. Her legs went around my waist as I leaned her back against the door. I pushed up her skirt as she fumbled with the front of my pants. I was so hard it hurt.

I needed.

I pushed aside the crotch of her panties and had just enough presence of mind to meet her eyes. She nodded and I drove into her.

She made a low noise, her body shaking with the effort to stay quiet.

Staring into her eyes, I covered her mouth with my hand and watched, waited for her response. All she did was twist against me, her eyes closing with a slow flutter of her lashes.

I needed.

I slammed into her again.

I hadn't had a chance to pull even a third of the way out before she was rising to meet me, her mouth moving against my palm, tongue teasing, teeth scraping.

Mine.

I couldn't speak. Through the door, I could hear the voices of my security team talking with Amber. If I spoke, they'd hear. So I thrust into her harder and faster, telling her with every stroke what I couldn't say out loud.

I needed.

Mine.

Over the barrier of my hand, her eyes opened, pleading in their pale green depths. I twisted my hips and angled my body until I slid directly across her clitoris. She shuddered around me.

Mine.

I needed. She needed.

That...just...like...

She came around me, wet and sweet and shaking, and I followed, emptying myself inside her, my anger draining away as I rested my forehead against hers for the few sweet seconds of oblivion our pleasure granted us.

It had only lasted a few minutes, the drama outside still playing through. A discreet knock at the door reminded me that I still had something I needed to deal with.

"Yes?" I grimaced as I pulled out. Fortunately, the paper towel Aleena had brought out for my hand was enough to clean me. She headed for the bathroom to take care of herself.

It was Amber and I had no doubt she knew we hadn't merely been taking care of my hand. Still, she kept her voice professional. "Um. Mr. Murphy would like to know how you want him to deal with Mr. Pence?"

I considered asking if killing him and dumping the body in an alley somewhere would be an option.

Sighing, I glanced at Aleena as she came out of the bathroom. Her face was flushed, but she looked otherwise collected.

She nodded at me that she was ready and I opened the door. She followed me out, keeping a professional distance between us.

Coolly, I stared at the man who now stood cuffed between two uniformed guards, then turned my gaze to my head of security. "What are my options?"

Chapter 4

Aleena

"So it was that easy." I stared at the wall. I rubbed my temples and murmured, "It almost feels like cheating." I'd had a headache since Mitchell had been led out of the office, and it hadn't let up even after we'd gotten home. I'd thought eating would help, but it hadn't.

"It's not cheating." Dominic sat behind me his arms wrapped around my waist. We'd settled on the couch after a simple dinner of last night's leftovers, my body automatically leaning into his. He made a low noise in his throat as he skimmed his lips up my neck. Then in a wry voice, he added, "And I wouldn't call it easy."

The bruise blooming on his cheek was still faint, but it would be live and in full color come morning. I'd given him ice at the office, but he'd taken the first blow on his cheekbone, the second on his jaw and the entire side of his face had been swollen. "I still can't believe he hit you," I said, shaking my head.

"Twice," he reminded. "I let him hit me twice."

"He still hit you and you still let him. Twice." I sighed, confused. "Why?"

"It made sense."

Slowly, I rubbed the base of my neck. This so wasn't helping my headache. "Okay. Just how do you figure it made sense to let him hit you?"

He took my hand and dropped it on my lap. A moment later, his fingers were massaging my neck, then working up, under my hair, to my skull. That did help my headache.

"Because I know guys like him." He sounded smug, but kept up the massage. "I couldn't just outright fire him, not the way things were. He might've tried to sue, claiming I'd never intended to really hire him, that I just did it to seal the deal and intended to fire him for some made-up reason. He thought he had me over a barrel. But once he'd been made aware of the company policy and signed the contract agreeing to it, I had a legitimate reason once he fucked up. I knew he wouldn't go quietly though, so I had to apply a bit more pressure. He attacked me. He got two punches in and then I defended myself. I have him on assault. That's going to look really bad on his record. He can either let this go and I'll be quiet about it." He shrugged. "Or I can get ugly about it. Which one do you think is going to work out better for him in the long run?"

Good grief. I shook my head. "You know, this corporate America world? It's a lot more cutthroat than I would have thought. And I never thought it was all cuddly bunnies."

"I can give you cuddling if that's what you want." He ran a hand down my shoulders and across my stomach, then up to palm my breast. His fingers sought out my nipple and began working it to a stiff, throbbing peak.

"That..." My voice hitched. "That's not cuddling, Dominic."

"No." He tugged again, sending jolts of pleasure straight through me. "But it can lead to it."

He continued to toy with me, teasing my nipple through the thin cotton of my shirt and bra. Staring hard at the flickering television screen, I tried to focus on whatever it was we'd started watching. I couldn't even remember. He liked to play these games, stroke me and work me to a fever pitch while we talked about work or some mundane things.

Clearing my throat, I asked, "Do you think this is going to affect things with *Devoted*?"

The images flickering on the screen made no sense and my breathing was beginning to sound terribly loud as he flicked the tip of his tongue against my ear.

"No." He curved his free arm around my waist and pulled me more firmly against him. I felt his cock against the small of my back. My pussy throbbed and I started to press my thighs together to relieve some of the tension.

"Don't." Dominic's voice was firm.

Groaning, I dropped my head back onto his shoulder.

He pinched my nipple hard and I gasped.

He went back to discussing business. "They

43

shouldn't have messed with Eddie. They knew he and I were talking. Had they left him alone, then I would have left them alone. They made their bed. Now they can lie in it. Besides, I doubt they'd want to risk looking bad for an asshole like Mitchell. I might not press charges, but enough people know what kind of man he is. Word will get around."

He began to unbutton the plain cotton shirt I'd put on when we'd gotten home. Underneath, I was still wearing the black silk bra I'd worn to work. I was no longer wearing matching panties since those had been soaked. For some reason, I'd decided not to bother with them at all when I'd traded my skirt for a pair of comfortable leggings.

I stared at his hands as he freed each button. The sight of his hands baring my skin was painfully erotic and once more, I went to cross my thighs, hoping to ease the ache building there.

"I told you, don't."

"Dammit, Dominic!" I put my hands on his thighs, my nails biting into his skin through his dress pants. He hadn't changed his clothes other than removing his tie.

"I want to see your pretty tits, Aleena." He made the comment in the same tone of voice he would have used if he'd been telling some guy behind a counter that he wanted to look at a watch. The same tone I'd heard him use at a restaurant when deciding on the red wine instead of the white.

It shouldn't have been so fucking hot.

He skimmed his hands from my breasts down to my waist and said softly, "There's a brunch on

Sunday. For *Trouver L'Amour*."

"I know." I rolled my hips back against him. I wanted him inside me. I didn't care that I'd had him only a few hours ago. I wanted him. Now.

"I'd like you to come."

He could have thrown a bucket of cold water in my face and it would have had less effect. I tensed, and his hands stilled. Slowly, I started to pull away. He let me go and I rose, crossing to stand in front of the window. I needed some distance.

Shivering, I wrapped my arms around myself and stared outside. Twilight was falling over Central Park, but I couldn't appreciate the beauty of it. An ache tried to choke me, drowning out the pleasure I'd just been experiencing.

I should've been happy about this, but I couldn't be. I was still dealing with the humiliation from the last party. Hell, screw that. I was still dealing with the humiliation from dealing with his mother and Penelope on a regular basis. Dealing with Mitchell Pence.

I was still struggling to deal with *all* of it.

And I hadn't even told Dominic that there was more.

Lately, people at *Trouver L'Amour* and some at Winter Business Holdings were beginning to look at me oddly. I'd been hired as his personal assistant, hired to run his personal life. While that coincided with his business life, I was more involved in those things than I used to be. No one told me, but I knew Fawna hadn't spent so much time at work with him, and certainly hadn't attended business functions

45

together.

People were beginning to realize we were involved.

And earlier today, he'd had me up against the door of his office in *Trouver L'Amour*.

I'd been too aroused, too caught up in him to think at first, but later, I wished I had told him to stop. If Amber didn't know for certain before, she'd certainly figured it out today, and I doubted if the security guards had bought my lame excuse of tending to Dominic's hand. It didn't matter that I'd only meant to give him the time he needed to cool off. What mattered was what had happened and what people were thinking of it. Of me.

Forcing myself to speak, I asked him softly, "Why are you asking me?"

For the longest time, he didn't answer, and I began to wonder if I wanted him to.

Finally, he sighed. His voice was just as quiet as mine. "Because I want you there."

"That doesn't really answer my question." Shivering again, I rubbed my arms. The touch of skin against skin startled me and I looked down, realizing for the first time that I was standing there with my shirt and bra open. I didn't even remember him opening my bra. I quickly fixed it, closed the front clasp and hurriedly did up the buttons on my shirt. "I don't have to go. It's a business function and you'll have a million people there asking questions and passing you cards. Basically, you need your assistant, but Amber's your assistant for the business, so she should go. But if you're asking me…" I shook my head, not wanting to put words in his mouth. I needed to hear them from him. "Dominic, *why* do you want me there?"

Tension rippled under his voice and I could hear the frustration as he replied, "Because I don't want my personal assistant there. I want to be there with the woman I'm involved with. I want you there, Aleena."

"And if I don't want to go?" I sounded terribly small when I asked. I *felt* terribly small. I knew he could hear my reluctance and I didn't want him to think it was him, especially after I'd pushed so hard for proof that he wasn't ashamed of me. I just didn't know if I was up to doing this again already.

"Then you don't go," Dominic said. He said it simply and calmly and there was no anger in his voice. "I can't force you to go and I would never try. But I *want* you there and I don't want you there as my assistant. I want you there as the woman I'm dating, Aleena."

My throat was tight. I thought about the way Penelope always looked at me. The way Dominic's mom looked at me. As if I'd somehow fucked my way into a life I didn't deserve. I thought about all the sidelong looks I'd been receiving over the past week. Penelope and Mrs. Snow weren't the only two who thought it.

"People know about us," I said abruptly. I turned to face him as I spoke, wanting to see his reaction.

He made a dismissive gesture. "Do you think I give a fuck?"

47

"*I* care." Crossing my arms, I took two steps toward him. "I don't want people thinking I got my job just because you're fucking me. I don't want people thinking you put me in this position because you wanted an easy piece of ass."

He rose from the couch, coming forward in a slow, lazy prowl. Fire danced in his eyes and I could see the anger I'd incited in him. He reached up and caught my chin, his grip almost painful. "Then go with me."

It was a dare. I could see it in his eyes.

"Let me show them what you are to me."

He backed me up against the window, his arms moving to cage me in. In the way it always did when he was near, my heart began to race. My skin overheated and I could barely breathe. Love and lust swept through me. He was a drug, an addiction and the need for him went straight to my core.

He bent low and pressed his lips to the delicate skin at the base of my throat. "Come with me, Aleena," he challenged me. "Let me show them what you are to me."

I couldn't have said no if I tried. Mute, I nodded.

I was helpless as he began to undo the buttons I'd just done up. The shirt fell away and my bra joined it a few seconds later. He made a noise like a growl when he pulled off my leggings and found me bare underneath, the sound making me instantly wet. When he straightened, I reached for his shirt, but he caught my hands with his.

"No," he said. "Not tonight." He kissed the tops of each hand.

I made a sound of frustration, but he just laughed. When he swept me up in his arms, I caught my breath. "What..." Swallowing a nervous laugh, I asked him, "What are you doing?"

"I'm going to show *you* what you are to me."

"Am I allowed to talk tonight?" I asked as he carried me into the room. Not one of our bedrooms, but the room we used when he wanted to tie me up. I often found it ironic, how much he loved restraining me considering how he tied me up emotionally as well.

He stood me on the floor near the bed. "You're allowed to talk," he said, answering my question.

He walked around me and cupped my breasts from behind. I could feel the brush of his clothes against my bare skin and shivered. With a soft chuckle, he tweaked my nipples, hard enough to hurt and I cried out, arching into his touch. I still didn't understand why my brain was wired the way it was, craving the thin pricks of pain that melted into pleasure, but I didn't need to understand it, as long as I had him.

"You're allowed to moan." He skimmed his hands down my torso to my hips, his fingers not quite brushing against the thin curls that covered my pussy. "You're allowed to scream." He nudged me toward the bed and I let him maneuver me onto the slick silk. "You're allowed to beg. In fact, I encourage it."

I lay face down, my nipples hard and throbbing as they pressed into the cool sheets. He fastened the leather restraints around my wrists, the interior fur soft against my skin. I was thankful he'd thought of that because, as much as I loved being restrained, I didn't want to go to work tomorrow with marks on my wrists. When he moved to my legs, he pulled them far apart, exposing every inch of me. Because of my height, and binding my hands close to the headboard, he had to extend the foot-post restraints as far as they would go before he could fasten them around my wrists.

When I was spread out before him and vulnerable, he bent over me and whispered, "You're allowed to come. As often as you want. Just know that I won't be stopping until I'm done."

Fuck. I hated when he teased me and made me wait, but I had a feeling this was going to be almost as torturous. I was usually ready to pass out after two orgasms.

He boosted my hips up and my breathing started to hitch as he shoved a wedge between my hips and the mattress, elevating my ass and taking some of the pressure off of my shoulders and chest.

"Do you remember what I told you I wanted to do to you?"

A thrill of excited fear went through me. "You've told me a lot of things."

His thumb traced the seam between my ass cheeks. "This was something specific. Very specific. And I think you know what I'm talking about."

The bed squeaked as he pulled away.

When he returned, I twisted my head around, trying to look at him, but I couldn't turn far enough. The sheets beneath me had been cool, but they were hot now. My entire body was hot, burning, craving...I was scared of what was coming, but at the same time, I wanted it. At first, I'd thought I wanted it only because Dominic did, but I realized now that I wanted it for me.

Something cool and wet dripped on my asshole and I flinched.

"Relax," Dominic said gently. He placed a hand on the small of my back and made soothing circles. "I'm just getting you ready."

"Are you...?" my voice cracked. I didn't think I was ready for this yet. I wanted it, but I wasn't ready.

"Not tonight, Aleena."

I wasn't sure which was greater, my relief or my disappointment.

"Tonight," he continued. "I'm going to ride you."

The words brought hot, blatant images to mind, but I still wasn't sure. He pushed his finger inside my ass and I gasped at the sudden pain.

"Push down," he instructed.

I squirmed and tried to twist away instead. I didn't know where I thought I'd be going, only that I wanted to get away from that intruding finger.

Immediately, he spanked me. *Hard.* The shock of it brought tears to my eyes.

"Did you hear me?" he demanded, his voice firm.

"Yes, sir," I managed.

"Then do it. Push down and take it," he said, pushing the tip of his finger against my ass again.

I whimpered...and then gasped, because when I did what he'd said, a delicious, hot sensation raced

51

through me as his finger penetrated me. He withdrew and then pushed forward again. This time, it didn't hurt. There was still a slight burn, but it didn't feel any worse than the place on my ass where he'd spanked me.

"That's my girl," he murmured. "Let me have you."

I didn't tell him that he already did. Body, mind and soul. I was his, whether I wanted to be or not. And right now, I definitely wanted.

"Such a good girl." The hand on my back slid up my spine and back again. "Letting me fuck your ass with my fingers. I'm going to use something else tonight, and then, I'll give you my cock."

I barely heard him as I moved tentatively back against his finger, not just letting him do it, but helping him. When he stopped, I mewled and twisted, trying to bring him back to me.

He held me still with one hand on my hip. "I'm going to give you something bigger than my fingers now." His voice was ragged, raw.

I nodded. I'd forgotten to be embarrassed, forgotten that good girls weren't supposed to like these sorts of things. All I cared about was him and what he was doing to me.

He pushed something blunt and thick against me and I made desperate little thrusts back with my hips, trying to bring it inside me despite the burn as it began to stretch me.

"Slow down, baby." He kissed the base of my spine as the object opened me wider. "Take it easy."

Easy? He expected me to take it easy as he

pushed something bigger than two of his fingers into my ass? It hurt, but it filled me and I needed that right now. He kept his hand on my hip, controlling the steady, agonizing movement until my body was shaking and he was done. I waited for him to move it, to do something to quench the ache inside me.

Instead, he moved around to the front of the bed, leaning over so he could see my face. "It's a plug," he said, heat glazing his eyes. "It's going to help you." He pushed the hair away from my face. "You have no idea how amazing it looks, your ring stretched around it. And knowing it's all to get you ready to take my cock..." His breathing hitched. "I could probably come just from looking at it."

"I..." Licking my lips, I shifted my hips, groaning as the plug moved inside me. It wasn't enough though. Not nearly enough. "I need more."

"You'll get it," he promised.

Then he disappeared from view.

I was acutely aware of everything. The sound of the water being turned on, then off.

His footsteps.

The creak of the door to the closet.

Footsteps again.

Then he was releasing me from the bed posts. I knew better than to move without his permission. I didn't even want to know what it would feel like to be spanked with the plug in my ass. He took a moment to caress my wrists and then my ankles.

"Sit up on your knees."

I obeyed, gasping as the plug shifted inside me again. He came around the front of me with a cuff in his hand. It was leather and fur-lined like the others, but not attached to anything.

"This will be easier if you can behave." He took my wrists and bound them together in front of me. "You're going to keep your legs spread just like you would if you'd still been tied, do you understand?"

"Yes, sir." I nodded.

"If you don't, I'll get the spreader bar, but it'll make turning you over more difficult, and I'd rather not have to interrupt what I'm doing."

I nodded again.

"You remember the word, Aleena?"

There was something in his voice that I didn't recognize, but I didn't question it. "Yes, sir."

He held up what I hadn't seen before. A collar. Not some leather and studs or spikes kind of thing, but it was still a collar. Black velvet with small silver loops at regular intervals around it.

"These are for attachments," he explained, touching each one. "It can be a leash for leading or pulling. A way to bind your neck to your legs and contort your body in ways you can't imagine." He reached out and lightly touched one of my nipples. "Or to connect to nipple clamps." His eyes slid down my body. "Or clamps in other places."

Oh, fuck.

"But that's for another time." He knelt on the bed in front of me, close enough that I had to tilt my head to look up at him. "I've never had a Sub I could teach like you. I've always just met up with women from the clubs or others who knew my...perversions," he said it softly, with a weird little smile. "But you..."

My breath hitched as he touched my mouth with his fingertips.

"Just how far can I take you, Aleena?" The need to hear it was clear on his face.

Licking my lips, I answered honestly, "I don't know. But I'm willing to find out."

His eyes blazed and he held up the collar. "I want to put this on you," he said. "But you need to understand what it means. Some Subs wear their own collars for decoration or as part of what they like, but it's different when a Dom gives one to a Sub, asks a Sub to accept one." His voice softened and, for a moment, his eyes slid away from me. "One like this, it's a sign of...ownership."

My stomach clenched but I didn't make a sound. I needed him to clarify.

He looked at me again. "I've never given a Sub a collar, because that would imply we had an understanding between us, that they were mine." His fingers rubbed across the velvet and I could almost feel the touch on my own skin. "But I bought this one for you."

Fuck.

"Will you accept it?"

I didn't hesitate, didn't stop to consider anything but the fact that he'd bought it for me. Only me. This was something no one else had of him.

"Yes."

His entire face lit up and, as he leaned forward to fasten the collar around my neck, he brushed his lips against my cheek. Before drawing back, he whispered in my ear, "Now, my darling, my beautiful girl, I want to take you *everywhere.*"

He climbed off the bed and stripped out of his clothes in only a few seconds. I had only a glimpse of his amazing body before he was behind me again. I felt something attached to the back of the collar and then felt something on my back. I had just enough time to realize it was a leash of some kind before he was bending me forward again, pulling the wedge out of the way so I was taking my full weight on my elbows.

Then he put his mouth on my exposed pussy and licked from top to bottom.

Being taken this way was different than anything I'd felt before and I keened, eyes closing as he held onto my hips, using his lips and tongue to send pleasure coursing through my body. He stabbed his tongue into me, his fingers digging into my flesh. I couldn't breathe as he drove it in again, then turned his attention to my clit. It was too much and I tried to twist away. The attempt was laughable.

Dominic's shoulders wedged me in place and in desperation, I tried to move against him. "Please...please...please..."

"Tell me what you want," he said. He pressed an open mouthed kiss on the inside of my thigh. "I'll give it to you. But you have to tell me."

"Make me come. Please, sir...please...please..."

He pushed two fingers inside me and scissored them. My pleas turned into a wail. I was too full. And then he pushed his thumb against the base of the plug in my bottom. I'd almost forgotten about it, the stretch and burn in the back of my mind until his touch moved things.

With a harsh groan, I came, but he didn't stop, his mouth devouring me even around words I could barely grasp. "That's it. You're soaking me, Aleena. Give me more...more..."

I was already shaking with the urge to come again and then he was leaning over me. Every nerve in my body was on fire, every sense heightened. I could feel his cock, hard against my back. Feel the wet dripping down my thighs. Smell the aftershave he'd put on that morning mingling with the scent of sex. The scent of me.

"Look at me," he ordered, tugging on the leash.

I let him pull me up on my knees again so that I could see him. My eyes caught movement and flicked down, watching him wrap his hand around his cock. Another tug and I looked up again.

"You came all over me, Aleena." The lower half of his face was glistening and I flushed as I realized why.

"I'm sorry, sir," I said.

"Don't be sorry." His voice was surprisingly soft. "I enjoy making you come, and those were particularly...delicious."

He leaned forward and pressed his lips against mine. I opened my mouth and tasted myself on his lips and tongue. He kept it brief, pulling back as he continued to stroke himself. I looked down again and I watched as the fat head of his cock disappear, then reappear, swollen and ruddy. I wanted it inside me.

"Now, Aleena, what do you want?"

Slowly, I looked up at him, surprised.

"You were very good and did as you were told. What do you want?"

I licked my lips and looked back down at his cock. "That."

He smiled, looking pleased with my answer. He nudged my back and I bent over again, quivering in anticipation.

As he started to press inside me, he groaned. "You're tighter. You feel it...don't you?"

Who was he fucking kidding? Of course I felt it. I felt everything.

He tugged on the leash. "Answer me."

"Yes, sir. Please, sir..."

"Good girl." He continued to tug on it, not hard, just enough to remind me that it was there. That I was his.

So good...so good...

I didn't even know I was talking, begging, pleading with him until he brushed his fingers across my mouth and said, "If you keep talking like that, this will be over before I'm ready."

He pressed his thumb against my lips and I bit him. He growled and slammed into me, hard, his pelvis pushing against the plug in my ass.

The lava-hot explosion of pleasure that coursed through me was so intense, I screamed.

He did it again.

And again...

"*Please!*"

He jerked on the leash. "Please *what*..."

"Please sir!"

I came again.

With one final thrust and a string of curses, he joined me. And as he slumped over my back, his hands sliding under me to cup my breasts, I heard him breathe my name.

***

Later that night, I climbed into my bed.

Alone.

We'd rested in the room for a while after he removed the restraints and the plug. He'd held me, rubbed lotion into my wrists. We hadn't talked, but that was okay. And then we'd gone our separate ways to shower and go to bed.

It felt odd to come in here alone after what felt like some of the most earth-shattering intimacy imaginable. My hand went to my neck where his collar had lain. It was back in the room, safely tucked away for the next time we were in there, but I could feel the ghost of it against my skin, as much a reminder as the ache between my legs of how much I belonged to him.

My whole body ached actually.

It wasn't a bad feeling, but I was sore and I would have loved to be able to curl up against Dominic and have him hold me through the night.

But that was only a dream.

Thinking back to everything that had happened over the week, to everything he'd told me and everything I now knew, I realized it was pretty close to a miracle that he could even *be* with me like this, that we were even having something close to a real relationship. The collar had been a huge deal for him, I knew, even though it only symbolized what we were sexually.

Still, I felt hollow, lying in my big empty bed alone.

I wanted to be with him.

In his bed.

Or mine.

Even in the bed he'd crafted solely for the purpose of sex.

I had a lot, more than what any other woman had ever gotten from him. I was greedy though.

I wanted all of him.

Chapter 5

Aleena

Nerves had turned me into a wreck.

For the fiftieth time, I smoothed down my skirt and then checked my make-up.

When I went to shut the compact, Dominic snatched it out of my hand and I watched, bemused, as he tucked it away. "Think you might need to powder your nose later, Dominic?" I asked, cocking an eyebrow. "I hate to say this, but I think you'd need a slightly paler shade."

"You're cute." He patted my knee and kept his hand there, his fingers squeezing lightly, a proprietary gesture that left me feeling warm inside.

"Since you don't need it, can I have it?" I smiled at him sweetly.

"You don't need it either."

He traced a pattern on the inside of my thigh. That light touch sent a shiver up my spine, but I refused to be distracted.

"Come on, Dominic, give me my compact."

He pretended to consider it and then gave me a

61

slow, slightly wicked smile. "You can have it for a trade."

"A trade?" I regarded him suspiciously.

"Yes." His fingers worked higher under the hem of the simple, but stylish black dress I'd selected for the brunch. "You can have it if you give me your panties."

I gaped at him. I scooted away so that his hand wasn't near anything important. I didn't, however, move completely away from his touch. His fingers lingered on my knee. "Not happening."

"What's the harm?"

"It's stupid, it's childish, and I'm not doing it." I gave him what I intended to be a scathing look. Based on the amused expression on his face, it hadn't worked. "You can't even give me a good reason other than being perverted." I allowed myself a smile to let him know it wasn't meant as an insult.

Dominic rubbed his thumb over the surface of the compact. "Penelope is going to be there. I imagine it would piss her off to know I was standing there with your panties in my pocket while I shook hands."

"That's..." I tried to ignore the stab of arousal that went through me. And the bit of vindictive pleasure at imagining the look on Penelope's face. I made my voice as disapproving as possible. "Now that's just plain juvenile, Dominic."

He shrugged. "I'm also right."

***

62

It took less than fifteen minutes after that to get to the offices of *Trouver L'Amour*. I climbed out, painfully aware of my nakedness under my dress. I'd chosen this one specifically because it was simple and would work for a multitude of occasions. It didn't hurt that it also hugged my curves and the neckline showed off just a hint of cleavage.

I'd seen the appreciation in Dominic's eyes when I'd come out of my room. I pulled that image to mind now as he helped me out of the car.

I can do this, I told myself.

He slid his arm around my waist and leaned in, kissing my temple. "Why are you so nervous? I can feel how tense you are." His breath stirred my hair. "It's not like you haven't been to these things with me before."

"But I haven't." I eyed the door and then slowed, turned to stare up at him. I shrugged and tried to laugh it off. "I've been to business functions. Aleena Davison, PA to Dominic Snow, has been to plenty of functions. But Aleena hasn't been to many things with Dominic. And nothing this big. That's...new. You asked me here on a date. This makes it our second big, public date and the first one was pretty much a bust. I know we went out to eat a couple times, but this...it's..." I shrugged again, feeling lame. "It's different."

Dominic was silent for so long that I turn my head to look at him. He was staring off into the distance past my shoulder. As though he sensed my gaze, he turned to look at me, blue eyes thoughtful.

He slid his hand up my spine and then curled his fingers around my neck. The gesture was utterly possessive and yet protective at the same time. Heat bloomed in my stomach...and other places.

"I think," he said, drawing each word out slowly as his fingers made small circles on my skin. "Maybe we should consider this our first date. The last one didn't go well and it was my fault. I should have had thought that through better. There was no way I could do the things I needed to do and still spend the time with you that you deserved for a real date. I'm sorry for that." His eyes darkened. "I need to do better and I know it."

His thumb brushed against the hollow under my ear and my heart skipped a beat. I reached up to touch him, to let him know that we were okay. That it was all okay.

But it wasn't.

He took a step back and I saw the anger in his eyes. It wasn't towards me though. All that emotion was directed at himself.

I reached up and touched his cheek, his faint stubble scraping against my palm.

"Dominic," I murmured. Hesitant, uncertain of what I wanted to say, I slid my hand higher and ran my fingers through his hair. "Don't blame yourself. We're both still new at this."

He didn't pull away again, but he didn't move closer either. "I'm supposed to take care of you." His voice was stark.

For a few brief seconds, I was so surprised at his

words that I didn't know what to think. I didn't know what to feel. And then the indignation came. "Take care of me?" I stiffened and pulled back my hand. "I don't need anybody to take care of me."

A faint smile tugged at Dominic's lips. A hint of arrogance tinged his voice. Arrogance and something I couldn't quite place. "That's what I do, Aleena. You're mine."

His words didn't change the entire tone of the moment, but it did give me pause. I took a deep breath and made myself think. We didn't have a typical relationship and I knew there was nothing about us that could be described as typical in any way shape or form, but I wasn't going to have him take me over, either. In some ways, I loved that he called me his, but in others, I didn't want him to think that I wasn't my own person.

"Look." I forced myself to think through each word, forced myself to consider everything I was feeling and thinking. "When we got into this, I knew it would be complicated, but you know me. Or, at least, I hope you do. By now, you should know me well enough to understand that I'm not a submissive. Not out here. It all stops at the bedroom door. I'm not going to stand by while you take care of things for me. You don't *own* me."

His hand was still curved around my neck, his eyes intense. I felt like he was staring straight through me, straight into my soul.

"Tell me something, Aleena." Dominic pressed his forehead against mine, the gesture strangely more intimate than many of the things we'd done.

65

"If somebody wanted to hurt me or harm me, would you let it stand?"

That was the last thing I expected to hear from him? And I didn't have an answer.

He didn't seem to need one. He brushed his thumb across my lip. "When I told you the truth about me, about what had happened, you took care of me." Now his voice was raw. "You and I both know that was what you did. That's what people who need each other do. They take care of each other."

He brushed his mouth across mine.

A shiver of warmth raced through me.

He didn't pull away, the words hot against my lips. "I didn't protect you that night and I'm not happy about that."

***

"You remember Joshua, don't you, Dominic?" Penelope gazed at Dominic with a coy smile as she leaned up against a man who might have been a model. He had the right look.

They had been two of the first to arrive, followed quickly on the heels of several others, but we'd managed to stay out of their path until now. I wished we could have avoided them longer, but they'd followed us onto the balcony.

Penelope ran a hand down the man's chest and leaned against him, but her eyes were on Dominic, not her pretty partner. They were dazzling together,

I had to admit. Okay, *he* was pretty dazzling—
Joshua. I don't think I'd ever seen a man that pretty.
And that was definitely the right word for him.

Ebony hair, wide green eyes so thickly lashed, I
could almost imagine him putting on mascara.

He smiled, but then he slid his gaze down to
linger on my breasts. I managed not to cross my
arms over my chest. The look left me feeling dirty.
And pissed off.

Dominic moved slightly in front of me and held
out his hand, a faint smile on his face. It wasn't a
nice smile. "I can't say I do, Penelope. Joshua."

Joshua accepted Dominic's proffered hand and I
watched as the man's face went slightly pale, his
mouth tightening. I glanced down and saw his
fingers being slowly crushed by Dominic's grasp. As
much as I would've liked to see the lecher's hand
broken, I couldn't let Dominic do it. Moving in, I
rested a hand on his upper arm. "Dominic," I spoke
softly, but it was enough.

The handshake ended abruptly. Penelope
laughed, and the sound was delighted. I managed
not to roll my eyes, but it took an effort.

She thought that little display was about her. It
figures.

Dominic flicked his eyes over at her as he shifted
his body toward mine, resting his hand at the small
of my back. His stance was close, protective.
"Penelope, you've already met Aleena. Joshua, this is
Aleena Davison."

"Dominic, really." Penelope made a disparaging
noise. She apparently had an entire symphony of

67

them. She sighed and shot me a dismissive look. "You need to stop working from time to time. Have a social life. Bring a date on occasion, not just your secretary."

Dominic smiled at her. Any anger I might have felt suffered a quick, abortive death as Dominic pressed a quick kiss to my temple. His fingers flexed on my back and I shivered.

His gaze was steady on Penelope as he spoke, "I did bring a date." He waited a moment to let that sink in, then he looked down at me, making it clear they were being dismissed. "We better go and mingle, make sure everybody's having a good time." He held out his arm.

I took it, a thrill going through me as he pulled me close enough to make it clear it wasn't merely a polite gesture. As we walked away, I could feel Penelope glaring daggers into the back of my skull.

I waited until we were some feet away before I said, "You do know that if looks could kill, Penelope would probably be getting arrested for murder very soon."

"It's a good thing looks can't kill." Dominic was smiling, but it was that cold one again. "That bastard would be dead too."

I didn't have to ask who he was talking about. I knew, no matter what I said, on some level, Dominic was still thinking 'mine'. This time, I didn't mind.

We stopped a few minutes later as he introduced me to another couple. There was speculation in the eyes of the woman, but the man greeted me warmly. We chatted for a few minutes and then moved on.

68

That seemed to set the tone for the evening. I would get curious gazes from some, cool glances from others while others would smile and seem perfectly interested in meeting me. I did catch a few men checking me out, but no one was as blatant or disrespectful about it as Joshua had been.

We'd been there maybe thirty minutes when another guest arrived and with it, the temperature dropped. Or so it seemed. Jacqueline St James-Snow took one look at me and scowled.

I didn't change my expression.

Her attention flicked toward Dominic and she gave him a regal nod, her face smoothing out.

That was the beginning and end of their interaction for the evening.

Anytime they accidentally ended up too close, one or the other would casually steer themselves in the other direction. I went with Dominic, of course, and by the end of the night was feeling vaguely dizzy.

I wanted to ask what was going on, but, despite how much Dominic had shared, I didn't feel comfortable asking. Besides, this was hardly the time and the place. I couldn't deny that part of my reasoning was selfish. I didn't want to worry about things that involved his mother or Penelope tonight. I only wanted to enjoy a real date with a man I knew I cared far too much about.

***

Trouver L'Amour's office were massive and sprawling, tucked inside a building that had probably a good dozen rooms that were almost impossible to find unless you actually worked in the building.

One of them was a private bathroom for the employees.

We'd been ready to head out and I'd ducked out ahead of Dominic to use the facilities while he hung back to shake a few more hands. There were still several couples around. Not Penelope and Joshua, but a few clients still lingered. Key personnel from management remained to handle things until all the clients were gone and Dominic wanted to make sure the management had a good example of what he expected. They, after all, would be responsible for things like this when he moved on from *Trouver L'Amour*. Nobody—including Dominic—seemed to know when that might be. It could be a few months or even a few years. He felt it was better to be prepared.

Inside the bathroom, I finished washing my hands and I checked my makeup. The glow on my face made me look strange. Almost unrecognizable. At least to me. I looked...

"Happy," I murmured, feeling a little dazed at the idea. How long had it been since I'd felt this way? Not once since coming to New York, not truly happy. There'd been a few moments snatched here and there, but nothing like this.

I might have followed that chain of thought more thoroughly, but the bathroom door opened and I automatically turned to look. The sight of Dominic ducking inside made my heart skip a beat.

"This is the ladies' room," I said, chiding him.

He didn't speak as he came up to me and grasped my shoulders. Without a word, he turned me so I was facing the sink and mirror. His eyes were two blazing jewels, bright and clear. He wrapped his arms around me and pressed his cheek against mine, the scruff rough against my skin.

He still didn't say a word.

His eyes held mine as he caught my hands and guided them into place on the polished marble vanity. There was enough distance that it left me bent slightly at the waist. He remained silent as he pulled the bottom of my dress up over my hips, leaving me with my ass thrust up and back toward him. I shivered as the cool air caressed between my legs. My thighs were already damp.

"I've been reaching in my pocket all night, feeling that bit of silk," he said softly, tracing patterns on my ass with his fingertips. "You know how many times I've looked at you and thought about you being bare under this, Aleena?"

When I didn't answer, he brought his hand down sharply on my ass.

I gasped out, biting my lip to keep from making any noise. Aside from instinctively knowing that he didn't want it, I didn't want anyone hearing us. As the sting receded, I whispered, "No, sir."

"Too many times." He put something down on the vanity next to my left hand.

The entire world narrowed down to that single

item.

It was a soft silicone plug. I didn't need measurements to know this one was larger than the last one he'd had in my ass. He'd used that one twice more since that first time and while it had still burned, I knew I'd feel a difference. This one wouldn't go in as easily. The sight of it made my heart race and my skin felt too tight, too hot, too small.

"You're not going to—"

Dominic said, "Be quiet, Aleena."

I swallowed and did just that. I knew better than to argue with that tone unless I planned to use my safe word.

He said nothing else.

The weighted silence added to the tension as he prepared me. And that's all it was, simple preparation. He didn't caress me, didn't play with me. He didn't kiss me or stroke me or any of the other things I'd come to associate with our sex life. He didn't even kiss me. I felt the cool slick of lubricant and then his finger was pushing past my ring of muscle. I took in a shuddering breath at the familiar painful pleasure. After just a few strokes, he added a second finger, scissoring the two until my fingers were curling against the cool marble. My legs were quivering and I almost protested when he removed his fingers, catching myself just in time. I heard the sound of him lubricating the plug and I was all but panting in anticipation by the time he was done.

My entire body was already shaking when he

pressed the rounded, blunt tip against my anus and gripped my hip with his other hand. "Don't make a sound, Aleena. Nod if you understand."

I gave a single, sharp nod, not trusting myself to move anything else. I was afraid I'd fall apart if I did, beg him for a real touch. His hand tightened for a moment and that was it.

He pushed the plug inside me.

I squirmed and shuddered and when it got to be too much, he backed off, giving me time to adjust before he pressed forward once more. Each agonizing inch seemed to last an eternity. My entire world consisted of the smooth stone under my palms, the hand on my hip and the narrow point where pleasure and pain met. When he finally had it settled inside me, he gave me another moment and then drew my skirt back down over my hips.

"Look at me."

I met his gaze in the mirror, catching a glimpse of my own wide eyes.

"How does it feel?" He curled his arm around my waist and rested his chin on my shoulder. His body was close to mine, but not flush against me.

Swallowing, I squirmed a little and then responded honestly, "Tight. Uncomfortable."

He slid his hands around my waist to rest on my stomach. "It's larger than the one I've been using. It's going to stay inside you on the drive home. And I'm going to fuck you while you're wearing it."

I bit my lip to keep from making a sound. I wasn't sure if it would've been protesting or begging. I didn't have the chance to analyze it though because he was taking my arm and we were walking out to the limo. Each step was agony, making the plug shift inside me. I could barely manage to walk normally. Only the fear that someone would see a change in my gait and figure out why, kept me moving in a natural way.

Then there was the ride home. It was...intense. Every bump, every slight movement of the limo jostled the plug. I hadn't lied before. It was tight and uncomfortable. And then things got really interesting. We'd gone maybe five minutes and something vibrated inside me .I jumped and gasped and shot Dominic a look. He was staring outside.

What the...

I looked back out my window, trying to calm my racing heart and wondering why he was trying to look so disinterested.

Thirty seconds later, it happened again. I whipped my head around to stare at Dominic. Hot, wicked blue eyes greeted me.

And the bastard was smiling. "Is something wrong?"

I gasped as it happened again. "What are you...?"

He lifted up his hand and he was holding something in it. As I watched, he pressed a button and it happened again. The plug inside my ass started to vibrate. It lasted longer this time. I was practically wailing when he stopped. I don't know if it was seconds later or minutes, only that I was shaking and clutching at the seat, a climax hovering just out of my reach. I wouldn't have thought it was

74

possible to come only from something in my ass, but I was so wet and desperate to come, I would have begged for it if I thought it would have done any good.

I turned to rest on my hip, unable to take any more pressure on the plug.

Dominic asked again, "Is something wrong?"

"You," I panted out. "Are an evil bastard."

"If you can keep from climaxing until we get home, I'll reward you." He pushed the button again and I clenched my thighs together and ground my teeth. It was going to be a long ride home.

I wasn't entirely sure how I'd managed to hold off my orgasm, but when the car stopped in front of the penthouse, I was a quivering mass of need, desperate for release. I was so focused on not coming that Dominic had to practically pull me out of the limo. My legs buckled and he wrapped his arm around my waist. It was all I could do to put one foot in front of the other and I was pretty sure I kept whimpering the entire walk to the elevator.

When the elevator doors slid shut behind us, I tilted my head back and whispered beseechingly, "Dominic, please."

He brushed his lips against mine in an almost-kiss. "We're almost there, baby."

"*I'm* almost there." I clutched at him, forgetting myself, forgetting everything but the need for release. I cupped him through his trousers. His body tensed and I heard him suck in a breath. I flexed my fingers, wanting to hear that sound again.

Instead, he caught both my wrists and walked

me back to the wall. He pinned my arms over my head, his mouth coming down on mine. I parted my lips, sliding my tongue into his mouth, curling it around his. He made a growling sound in the back of his throat as I drew his tongue into my mouth, sucking on it. And then he was pulling back. I tried to follow, but he was too tall, able to hold me in place while denying me what I wanted.

"Greedy, greedy Aleena," he said, his voice rough.

"Damn straight." I writhed against him, desire turning my body into one giant nerve ending. I needed him.

The elevator came to a stop and the doors slid open on a whisper. I made a sound of protest as he released me. The walk from the elevator to inside the penthouse was a blur and when the door closed behind us, I turned to him, squirming, my body half-tensed for another jolt from the plug while everything in me readied for climax, or whatever form of torture he had ready. It didn't matter, as long as I didn't have to wait anymore.

He moved to stand in front of me and I held still as he slowly stripped me naked. Like in the restroom, the removal of my clothes was almost detached. Unzipping the dress and peeling it off without touching my skin. My bra joining the dress on the floor, but no attention paid to my breasts. The inside of my thighs were dripping and I flushed as I wondered if I'd left a wet spot on my seat in the limo.

Damn him and his games.

"On your knees."

I went down automatically.

"Open my pants. Take me out."

"Yes, sir." I swallowed hard and followed his orders, my hands shaking. I was still awkward at this, but I licked my lips in anticipation, remembering the feel of him in my mouth, the weight and taste of him on my tongue. I leaned forward, eager to feel it again, but he grabbed my hair and stopped me.

"Did I tell you to lick my cock, Aleena?"

"No, sir."

I looked up at him and saw the expression on his face. He was in the mood to play with me today. Fine. I could play. "But you said I could have a reward." I made my voice as sweet as possible.

Something dark and primal flashed through his eyes. He brushed his knuckles against my cheek. "Are you saying that having my cock in your mouth is a reward?"

"I'm saying anything with you is a reward." When I leaned forward this time, he didn't stop me and I opened my mouth, took him inside.

He groaned, the hand in my hair tightening painfully.

I took him deep and felt him shudder.

A stab of pride went through me. Knowing I could make a man like him feel this way – it was definitely a reward.

I wrapped my hand around the base of his cock as I focused on the few inches I could take comfortably. I circled the head with my tongue, teasing the tip before sucking on it, repeating it several times before slowly taking all of him, my body fighting the need to gag. I cupped his balls, caressing the soft skin, bringing him close, so close. I could feel it in the way the vein along the underside of his cock pulsed against my lips. I could hear it in the way his voice all but rasped out my name.

And then he was dragging me up.

I barely had time to register being on my feet before he had me bent over, my hands braced on the low coffee table, his hands gripping my hips.

He drove inside me, hard and fast. He was buried so deep inside me I could barely breathe. Everything else around me was gone as every fiber of my being focused on where our bodies joined. I was so full. Too full. It should have hurt, but my body was throbbing, unable to figure out if what it was feeling was pleasure or pain. Then his hand twisted in my hair and he jerked me up. It was an awkward angle and his grip on my hair send pinpricks of pain through my scalp.

"You're so fucking tight," he said in my ear as he pulled out, slowly, then surged back in, making me gasp. "I can feel how full you are. You were tight before, but this...you're like a vice, baby. Can you feel it?"

"Yes." I could barely process the question.

His hand came down on my ass and I cried out.

"Yes, what?" he demanded.

"Yes, sir. Yes, sir!" The answer came automatically.

He spanked me on the other cheek and I

bounced up on my toes, gasping as the vibration rippled through me. My pussy tightened and Dominic hissed. His fingers tightened on my hip as he withdrew, then pushed back in, rocking his hips in a slow rhythm.

"I love the way you move." His hand slid around my stomach and then lower, fingertips skimming down only to stop just above where I wanted him.

"Please," I gasped, pushing back against him.

I was rewarded with another smack to my ass and my back arched. Fuck.

"You like it when I spank you, don't you, baby?"

"Yes..." I waited a second too long. Then added, "Sir."

He spanked me again and I came, crying out my pleasure as it burst over me.

"That's my girl."

He took me to the floor on my hands and knees and started to ride me hard and fast, with deep, brutal digs of his cock that drove the screams from my throat even when I didn't have the air in my lungs to muster sound. The angle allowed each thrust to press the plug deeper, sending another jolt of pleasurable pain through me and sending wave after wave of ecstasy through me until I didn't know where one climax ended and another began.

It was too much and not enough. I couldn't handle anymore but I didn't want him to stop.

I heard Dominic swear in a low, heavy voice and then...nothing.

Chapter 6

Dominic

I've had intense sex before and I'd been with women I taken well past the point. I'd watched as they blacked out and felt satisfaction at a job well done, a reputation upheld.

None of them had ever left me feeling the way Aleena did.

Maybe that was why I was still curled around her on the couch at two in the morning.

She was sound asleep.

I was far from it and she was the main reason why.

Turning my face into her hair, I told myself I'd do better if I got up and moved into my bed, but lying there with her...it was like nothing I'd ever experienced before. For the first time in as long as I could remember, I wasn't restless. With a start, I realized what I was feeling.

Peace.

I didn't want to give that up, and so I didn't

move. Besides, in a few hours, I'd have to be up and around, dealing with work and all the bullshit that came with it. And then there was other shit that would happen this week.

I shifted into a more comfortable position, my heart skipping a beat as she automatically curled into me. Yeah, I wasn't going anywhere any time soon, even if it meant staying awake all night.

***

I'd overslept.

The last thing I remembered doing was deciding I'd rather lie on the couch with Aleena and not sleep than get up and go to my room.

Somehow, I'd ended up falling asleep, my body wrapped tightly around hers. I'd only gotten a few hours of sleep, but they'd been the calmest, most restful hours I'd had in a good long while. Probably not since before my life had been turned upside-down nearly fifteen years ago.

Considering what I had coming up in just a few minutes, it was a good thing I'd slept well.

For a moment, I wished Aleena was with me, but then I pushed that thought out of my mind. She was my personal assistant and had more important things to do than stand around in my office all day. Right now, she was meeting with Annette out at the house to start picking out furniture. After some discussion, Annette had decided she wanted to do the house first, then the penthouse. Part of me wished I'd hadn't decided to do the redecorating now. I had enough going on and didn't need anything else to worry about, but it was too late to change the plans now. Besides, Aleena and Annette would be handling most of it, and if I was completely honest with myself, it was Aleena's absence I minded the most.

"Mr. Snow?"

I looked over at the doorway where a tall, slim blonde was standing. She was probably in her forties though she looked a bit younger. I couldn't remember her name. Amber had hired her to take over the assistant's position at *Trouver L'Amour* and it was her first day. The goal was to have her trained and confident so that when I hired someone to run the company in my place, she'd be able to help him. I never stayed in one position very long. I got bored far too easily.

She smiled at me politely. "Your nine-thirty is here."

"Thank you..." I wracked my brain for her name, but couldn't come up with it. "Show him back, if you would."

She nodded and walked away.

Moving back to my desk, I studied the file I had in front of me. It was pitifully thin. All the money I had and this was what I'd been able to come up with on my own. Then again, money was good for hiring professionals, thus, my nine-thirty appointment. I hadn't wanted to risk doing this at the penthouse where my mother or Aleena might stop by unexpectedly.

"Mr. Kowalski, sir."

Stanley Kowalski stood in the doorway, a skinny man with a thin face, eyeglasses perched on a thin nose. He wore a modest suit of a boring shade of gray and his smile was just this side of bland. For a moment, I was disappointed. I'd asked around. This man had come highly recommended.

Then he came toward me, hand outstretched. "Mr. Snow, it's a pleasure to meet you."

I gripped his hand and stared into his eyes. His eyes, unlike his smile, his suit, his demeanor, weren't bland. They were sharp and filled with a burning sort of intelligence. I gave his hand a quick shake and decided I'd withhold judgment. For now. We'd see how things went before I made a final decision.

***

"This isn't much to go on." Kowalski had gone through everything I'd given him, studied his notes and then turned his attention to me.

We'd been speaking for an hour and he'd asked what felt like a thousand questions, each of which I'd answered the best I could. Now it came time for *my* questions.

"I know," I said. "The question is, can you do it?"

He gave me a grin. It wasn't smug, but it was confident. He leaned forward, elbows braced on his knees. "Mr. Snow, I've found much more based on much less. I can't promise to find answers, but I can promise to do my best and if I can't find your birth mother, I can pretty much guarantee that nobody can. I'm usually considered a last resort in cases like these."

"Okay." I gave him a slow nod. "How do we get you started?"

He named a fee that was surprisingly low.

"That's the deposit. It's non-refundable."

He continued to watch me. No doubt he'd investigated the place, my name. Me. It's what I would've done if I'd been him.

"Then there's an hourly fee, including expenses. I'll be sure to give you clear reports—"

I waved a hand, not needing to hear the details. "You do what you have to. I'll get you my assistant's information. She'll go over the reports and check in with me. If you ever need to see me personally, you'll go through her to set up an appointment." I didn't mention that I needed to tell her about him first.

"Very well." He reached into his briefcase and pulled out a few papers. "There's a contract you'll have to sign. Legalities. You understand."

"I do." Then, because I wanted to take care of it before it became an issue, I added, "Please leave my adoptive family out of it unless you have no other choice. Especially my mother. She might have information, but try not to bring her into this unless there's no other choice."

"Of course." The expression on his face said that he understood all too well why I was asking. He definitely had experience in this sort of thing.

***

I gave up working two hours later. I'd gotten basically nothing done and knew the rest of the day would be equally as unproductive. I had too much on my mind and too little ambition to fight through my lack of focus.

I called one of my drivers and had him bring the car around. I had Maxwell driving Aleena mostly now. Times like these, I missed him, but I preferred knowing that he was taking care of her.

Rather than going back to the penthouse, we headed towards the Hamptons. I managed to make a few more calls on the ride, hoping we'd get to the house before Aleena and Annette left.

As we pulled into the driveway, I saw that I'd timed it perfectly. Annette and Aleena were coming outside. When they caught sight of my car, both women smiled. While they were both beautiful, only one of them managed to make my heart trip sideways and the blood rush straight to my cock, leaving me hard and aching with just that one look.

"I was hoping I'd catch you." I tried to keep my voice casual as I climbed out of the car.

I didn't fool her. She frowned as she walked towards me. "Is everything okay?"

I nodded and reached out to slide my hand down her arm, my fingers lingering on her hand.

Just the simple physical contact was enough to ease some of the tension in my chest.

"We're wrapping things up," Annette said, a knowing look on her face. She glanced down at her phone. "I hope you don't need me to walk you through the plans, Dominic. I've got another client meeting me in an hour on the other side of Manhattan."

"No, you're fine. Aleena can bring me to speed." I hoped I didn't sound too eager for her to leave.

Based on the smile, Annette saw right through me, but she didn't call me on it. Instead, she gave a general farewell and hurried to her car. In just a matter of minutes, Aleena and I were alone on the lawn.

"Were you planning anything after this?" I asked her.

"No." She brushed an imaginary wrinkle out of my suit.

I brushed a stray lock of her hair back behind her ear, wondering if she felt the same compulsive need to touch me as I did her. "Then would you have lunch with me?"

"Sure. Where do you want to go?"

I gestured up to the house. "In there. I'm having it delivered." I quickly added, "There are some things I want to tell you and I don't want to do it in public." I hoped she'd trust me enough not to be offended.

"Of course." She threaded her fingers through mine and led the way back into the house.

***

She listened.

Without question, without comment, she listened.

And when I was done, she came around the table to me.

There were empty cartons of food on the table and I was surprised I'd managed to eat at all. I'd ordered Chinese because I knew she liked it and food preparation wasn't the main thing on my mind at the moment.

As she walked towards me, I pushed my chair back from the table, turning it slightly so I could face her. She nudged my knee with hers and I obliged by spreading my legs so she could step between them. I reached up and grasped her hips, sitting up as I pulled her closer until I could actually wrap my arms around her, using the warmth of her body to center myself.

"I think you're doing exactly what you need to do," she said as she ran her fingers through my hair.

"Am I?" I closed my eyes, enjoying the sensation of her fingers against my scalp. "That's what I told myself for the longest time. But Mom, she's..." I grimaced at the word. That could get confusing. "Jacqueline, I mean. This is going to hurt her. I don't want that."

"She raised you. It's obvious she loves you."

I could hear the tension in Aleena's voice as she spoke about my adoptive mother.

88

She continued, "I don't much care for her, but I can tell she loves you, even if she does have a shitty way of showing it. I'd be surprised if you *did* want to hurt her."

"She's been a bitch to you."

"Plenty of people are unkind, Dominic." She shook her head. "You don't repay or fix that kind of deep, inbred wrong by repaying it with more of the same. Dark can't drive out dark, as the saying goes."

I slid a hand down her back and over her ass. I felt her stomach contract as she sucked in a breath. I kept moving down over her skirt until I hit the hem and then stroked back up her thigh, moving under the skirt this time to toy with the lace on her stockings. "Where in the world did you come from? People don't think like you."

"Sure they do." She cupped my face in her hands, tipping my head back so that I was looking up at her. She bent her head and pressed her lips against mine in a quick kiss. "I knew plenty of people like me back in Iowa. And I've met plenty here in New York. You just need to know where to look."

My hand tightened on her thigh. She was the most amazing woman I'd ever met and I wondered what I had done to deserve her.

"You're so sad, Dominic." She traced my mouth with her fingers. When she leaned down, I closed my eyes, breathing in the scent of her hair and the warmth of her skin. "Let me make you feel better." She lightly bit the top of my ear. "Sir."

I could barely keep my voice from betraying the

way my heart pounded against my ribcage. "What did you have in mind?"

I sat passively as she slid to her knees and reached for my belt. Without a word, she loosened my belt, opened the button, and slid down the zipper. As I watched, she reached into my pants and wrapped her hand around my already-swollen cock. "You didn't let me finish the other night."

"What a selfish bastard."

The last word was choked off as she took me into her mouth, her hand stroking the part she couldn't get in. When she pulled back, my cock was glistening with saliva, thick and heavy with need. Her hand worked me up and down until skin slipped against skin and then she lowered her head again.

I couldn't take my eyes off of her, no matter how much I wanted to close my eyes and just enjoy the sensation of that wet heat and the nearly unbearable suction of her mouth. When she took me all the way, my hands curled around the arms of the chair, fighting the urge to thrust. I knew I was technically still in control, but dammit all if she wasn't close to taking it. Then she hummed and the vibrations shot straight through me.

Fuck.

I didn't want to come in her mouth. I needed her. Needed to be inside her. Nothing between us. Skin against skin.

I reached down to give her hair a light tug. She raised her head and gave me a questioning look, the tip of my cock still in her mouth.

"Stand up and take off your underwear." My

voice was ragged.

She looked a bit disappointed, but she did as she was told.

I caught her hips. "Straddle me."

The look she gave me was hesitant, as if she wasn't sure what to do next. I tugged her closer, guiding her into place until the head of my cock brushed against her thighs. She reached beneath her to hold me steady and then began to sink down. My eyes locked with hers as she took me slowly, giving her body the time needed to adjust to the intrusion without preparation.

It was deeper this way and her weight drove me deeper than I'd been before. It was also impossibly intimate, which was why I never did it this way. She moved her hips tentatively, testing. Her face was only inches away and I could see that her lips were swollen slightly from what she'd been doing.

I had a million things inside me that I wanted to say to her in that moment, but I said none of them. Just guided her hips into slow, easy circles and stared into her eyes. She moaned low in her chest as the motion put the right kind of friction on her clit. I tugged her closer and took her mouth in a hungry, desperate kiss. She clung to me as I scraped my teeth along her bottom lip, as my tongue explored every inch that I was coming to know so well.

She moved harder and faster and I buried my face in her hair, not wanting her to see on my face what I couldn't say.

She came with my name on her lips and as I followed, I silently spoke the secret I wasn't yet

ready to tell her.
I think I love you...

Chapter 7

Aleena

"Whoa...look at you!"

I looked down at myself and then up at Molly, confused. "What?"

Molly grinned and patted the seat next to her. "I'm just...you look so happy."

"Oh." Flushing, I slid onto the booth next to my friend and shrugged. "I guess. Well, yeah." She leaned over and gave me a hug. I returned it, feeling a pang in my chest. I hadn't seen her in almost a month and I only just realized how much I missed her. "How've you been?"

"Okay. School sucks. Work sucks. I want a better job, but I need to get through school for that to happen...and the wheel just goes round and round." Molly shrugged, wrinkling her nose. Her dark eyes were dancing, telling me that things were actually fine. "How about you? How's life with the billionaire?"

I smacked at her arm. "Life with Dominic is good."

"Dominic." Her grin widened. "So how *is* Dominic? I mean, really. Give me details. Is he hung? How big is he? How does—"

"Hello, ladies!" A bright-eyed, cheerful server appeared at their section of the counter. "Can I get you something to drink?"

Molly started to snicker. I jabbed her in the side and ordered a soft drink. Molly ordered tea and as soon as the server left, she broke into fits of laughter.

"Sometimes you act like a twelve-year-old boy," I said, shaking my head. There was no malice in my words though. As embarrassed as I was by my friend's direct questions, it was nice to have someone to talk to.

Molly just grinned at me. "Come on. Let's figure out what we want to eat. We've got a couple of hours, right? I thought we could walk around and do some window shopping later."

***

"Oh, hey, sorr—" Shit. I stared at the woman Molly and I had almost run over as we came out of the diner. "Penelope."

I heard Molly make a noise next to me and hoped she wouldn't do anything crazy.

Penelope stood with another woman, this one

94

nearly a copy of Penelope herself, although I doubted she and Penelope were related. It was just that they seemed to have been cut from the same cloth. Hair expertly styled and colored. Eye makeup of a similar palette. Discreet pearl necklaces. Clothing choices were soft, pale pastels of course. The most tasteful colors only. Penelope wore pink while her friend wore a spring like shade of green. Even their shoes were similar. Beige pumps.

Penelope gave me a look of pure disdain and then took a step to the side as if to go around me. That's when she caught sight of Molly in her torn-up blue jeans and oversize t-shirt. Penelope's lips pursed and that made a decision for me.

I stuck out my hand to the other woman and gave her a polite smile. "Hi. I'm an...acquaintance of Penelope's. We met through Dominic. I'm Aleena."

The other woman glanced at Penelope as if for permission while I kept my hand out and the smile on my face.

"Dominic?" the woman finally said.

"Yes. He and I are dating."

The woman blinked and then looked over at Penelope. I didn't need to be a mind reader to know that the wheels were turning.

"Ignore her, Olivia," Penelope said, her mouth twisting into an unattractive smile. "You know Dominic wouldn't be caught dead dating somebody like that."

I felt Molly tense beside me, but I just laughed. "Oh? I guess that's why you keep getting seen at all the hot events with him." I hooked an arm through

Molly's and said, "Come on, Moll. Let's get back to shopping. I need an outfit for a party Dominic and I are attending."

***

"Are we going to a party?"

Dominic was waiting for me when I got back, an unreadable expression on his face.

"Ummm...." *Crap. How did he hear about it? How did he hear about it already?* Striving for a bright smile, I said, "I don't know. Are we?"

He came around the counter, a glass of scotch in his hand. "According to Penelope, we are. She called my mother and then my mother called me, pissed off and wanting to know why I'm attending a party with my *secretary*." He looked down at his scotch, amused. "Then she wanted to know where the party was and why she hadn't been invited."

I pressed my lips together. I was glad he seemed more entertained than angry, but I wasn't sure how he would take the whole truth.

He lifted his scotch to his lips and sipped, eying me expectantly.

I sighed. Spinning away, I moved over the couch and flopped down on it. "Molly and I ran into Penelope at the mall, almost literally, and she was being a bitch. I didn't plan on saying it. It sort of popped out."

He settled down beside me and put his arm

around my shoulders. As he pulled me close, he turned his face towards me, pressing it into my hair. I loved when he did that. It somehow seemed more intimate than other things we'd done. I snuggled into him, breathing deep the spicy scent of his aftershave, mingled with the smell of him.

"Why don't you tell me what happened?" he suggested, his fingers making soothing back and forth motions on my upper arm.

So I did. All in all, it took less than five minutes, starting from the time we left the old, fifties-style diner to when we bumped into Penelope. I finished with a shrug. "I didn't plan to say anything to her," I repeated. "But she has this way of bringing out the worst in me."

"It's a gift she has," he told me, wryly.

"It's not a pleasant one."

Chuckling, Dominic agreed with me. Then, he said, "I think we should have a party. A dinner party." He slid his fingers under the neckline of my shirt, his touch hot against my skin. "A dinner party here. I'll invite some of my friends. You invite yours. I'll even invite my mother and Penelope."

I frowned. "Is this a punishment?"

He laughed again and then, before I could blink, he'd rolled us both and had me under him. I moaned in pleasure at the weight of his body on mine.

"No," he said. "It's just clever thinking. She'll keep pushing until she knows we'll push back. So we'll give her a shove and she'll wish she'd kept her mouth shut." He bent his head and caught my lip, biting down lightly. "But if you'd like me to punish you..."

Yes, please. I shivered. "If you think you should, sir."

***

I got a crash course in party planning that week. It was Tuesday and he decided he wanted to have the party on Friday. Thanks to having worked with Fawna on the masquerade ball back in February and working with Amber on the *Devoted* event, I'd already figured out that while Dominic might know that he wanted to make things happen, he wasn't particularly good at the specifics. Hence why he needed an assistant.

If I could help put *those* events together, I could handle a small get together for a group of twelve. Well, fourteen, including Dominic and me. Invitations were easy. He gave me a list of people and I included Molly since she was my only friend. I was grateful to see Fawna's name on the list as well. I wouldn't have felt comfortable inviting her as one of my friends, but I considered her one. Knowing she and Molly would be there helped me relax a bit. Even though Penelope and Dominic's mom would be present, I had people who'd support me.

The meal? That wasn't so easy, but I begged and pleaded with Francisco and he agreed to come in and prepare. Actually, I didn't need to do much pleading. Francisco was actually delighted to help.

He'd confessed more than once that he didn't think Dominic truly appreciated his culinary skills.

Appetizers, wine, dishes...my head was packed with a million little things that no one ever thought about when preparing dinner for one.

By the time Friday rolled around and I was standing in front of the mirror staring at my reflection, I was kind of wishing that Molly and I had opted to see a movie for our girl day instead of a meal and window-shopping. We could have avoided the encounter with Penelope, which meant no dinner party...and I wouldn't have been wearing this.

It was pretty, yes, but Dominic had wanted to go for casual since he was having this in his place with friends and family. No, the outfit wasn't fancy, but it was sexy as hell and I felt more than a little self-conscious now. Wrapping my arms over the bared midriff, I looked back at my closet and debated. Maybe I should find something else. I was sure I had something I could throw together.

"You look beautiful."

Dominic stood in the doorway, the heat in his eyes at odds with the casual way he was leaning against the doorframe.

Turning away from him, I went back to staring at my reflection. The straps were all lace. My breasts and the upper part of my belly were covered by silk, but the bottom hem of the top was covered with jagged bits of scalloped lace that ended a good inch and a half above the waistband of crocheted lace at the top of my skirt. It was sweet and sexy and feminine. I loved the outfit and if it had been just for me and Dominic, I wouldn't worry.

But...

He moved up behind me and curled his arms around my waist. His nose brushed against the side of my neck as he pushed my hair aside. His lips pressed against my throat and he murmured, "You look incredible, Aleena."

"I don't fit." I covered his hands with mine, noticing more than ever how much darker my skin was than his. I was light for my heritage and he had a tan, but there was still a difference.

Dominic studied my reflection. "What do you mean you don't fit?"

"Just that. Penelope, your mother. Most of the women you know wouldn't be caught dead wearing something like this. No matter what I wear, no matter what I do, I'm never going to fit in with them." I felt foolish. And mad. What did I care what other women thought? What did I care if I fit in here? I'd never planned to do it, never thought I could. But still, my voice sounded terribly small as I said, "I don't know why I care. I shouldn't. I know that. But you..."

"You don't fit in." Dominic's voice was soft. He moved one hand up and cupped my chin, raising my head and forcing me to stare at my reflection. His golden head dipped low and I shivered as he ran his lips down the skin obscured by the lacy straps of my top. "You stand out. You blow my mind, Aleena."

My heart twisted at his words.

He turned me to face him, bringing his hands up

to cup my face. "Why would you want to fit in with women who find it amusing to belittle everybody who isn't them? Why would you want to fit in with people who are so caught up in who they are, they don't care how many people they've walked on to get where they are? Or how many people they walk on to stay there?" His lips caressed mine, taking my breath away. "Don't fit with them. Be you."

***

Fawna found Molly and me in the kitchen. She took one look at the wine we were drinking and shook her head. "I think I hate you both right now."

I lifted my glass and said, "Pour yourself some. There's more."

"I'm doing that." She made a beeline for the open bottle of red and gave Molly a friendly smile. "It's nice to meet you, Molly. I've heard a lot about you."

Molly tipped her glass in Fawna's direction. "Same here. I think I heard your name probably two thousand times the first few weeks she was working for the beast out there."

I glared at her. "He's not a beast."

"He's a sexy beast," Molly said, smiling at me as I shot her another dirty look. Then she took a healthy gulp of her wine. "But I couldn't work for him. I think he'd drive me crazy."

"Dominic would drive most women crazy."

Fawna gave her an understanding smile and the three of us settled against the counter to stare out into the living room. From where we stood, we had a bird's-eye view of the dinner party as it died a slow, natural death.

Penelope was there, and she'd brought Joshua. She hadn't stopped crawling over him all night and I was surprised he still had his shirt on, rumpled as it was. She hadn't even bothered trying to be discreet with her long, aggressive kisses. If anything, she seemed to want the attention focused on them. And through it all, she gave Dominic sidelong looks, as if to say, *See, see! He wants me...aren't you going to stop us?*

Jacqueline had already left. The ice in the air around her had been enough that I'd almost left to get a sweater to throw on over my outfit. I hadn't wanted to give her the satisfaction though. Especially not after the look she'd given me when she'd shown up, dressed in a semi-formal black sheath that went sedately down over her knees. She'd looked at Dominic in his jeans and sweater, then at me and made the comment, "I wish you'd informed me of the dress for the evening, Dominic."

She hadn't spoken to me all night, but she had come. I just wished I knew what that meant.

There were a few other people I knew vaguely there, several of whom I had only talked to on the phone. Almost all of them had been kind, friendly even.

The only two who hadn't been...well, let's just say it hadn't exactly been a surprise.

Joshua hadn't been friendly or unfriendly. There was no doubt he was mostly there to play at being Penelope's arm candy and occasionally try to cop a feel. She'd smacked him three times by the time the meal had ended.

I wondered if she had any idea that throughout the meal, Dominic had been amusing himself by stroking me...in a far more intimate manner and place. My silk panties were soaked, my body wired.

"Well, this went over better than I'd—"

Fawna's words ended abruptly when a crash came from the living room.

It was followed by a low, feminine sob and the three of us rushed out. Penelope was sitting on the floor behind the couch, clutching at the front of her shirt. Joshua was sprawled flat on his back next to her, a hand over his eye.

Dominic was rubbing his fist, looking furious as he glared down at Joshua as if deciding the best way to eviscerate him.

Penelope's eyes landed on me. Dominic wasn't looking at her so he couldn't have possibly seen the way her eyes narrowed slightly, or the way her lips curled.

But I did.

So did Molly. I thought Fawna saw it as well, but the three of us stayed silent, waiting to see what would happen next.

A moment later, Penelope got to her feet and rushed to Dominic, flinging herself at him and sobbing against his chest.

***

Twenty minutes later, he looked at me over her bent head. She was still crying, into a handkerchief now. He'd pulled it out of his pocket and given it to her and Fawna had guided her over to a chair while Dominic called for building security. Every time he tried to go more than a couple feet from her, she'd start making these little hurt noises until he was close again.

Molly and I leaned against the wall, watching the whole tableau.

"She's good," Molly said softly.

I nodded, crossing my arms over my chest. "Very."

Then I felt bad. Dominic had seen what had happened and had given us the short version.

Joshua had been tossing back the bourbon all night and had gotten so plastered, he'd barely been able to walk to the door. At some point, he'd decided that Penelope had teased him long enough. He'd made a pass at her again, grabbing at her breasts, and when she'd pushed him away, he hadn't gone. Penelope had ended up crushed between him and the couch. Her shirt was ripped at the sleeve and Joshua would probably feel like he'd been hit by a mack truck.

Through sobs, she'd announced that she didn't want to press charges, going pale at the very idea. Dominic had instructed security to get Joshua into a cab, but not before he'd made it clear to the dazed young man that if he ever saw his face again, he'd end up in the hospital rather than the police station.

Everybody else had trickled out except for Molly, Fawna and me. And our damsel in distress. A few more minutes passed before Penelope's sniffles eased.

"I'll have a car brought around." Dominic patted her shoulder. "We'll get you home."

She started to reach for him, then let her hand fall away. "Would you..." She darted a glance at me and for the first time, she managed a weak smile. "Oh, never mind. I couldn't ask. Really."

Oh, brother. Who was she kidding?

Dominic stared straight ahead, his expression unreadable.

"How about I ride home with you, Penelope?" Fawna asked.

I could have hugged her.

"Oh, no." Penelope stared at her, wide-eyed. "You have to get home to your little grandson. I heard you talking about how you worry so. With a teenaged girl watching him, you must be so stressed about that."

Dominic dipped his head and I could all but see the strain building inside him. "I'll take care of it, Fawna."

"But—"

He shot her a look and shook his head. "It's in the opposite direction of where you're heading and you already have a good forty-five minute drive."

His gaze came to me.

I saw the apology there and managed a smile I

didn't feel. I was better than Penelope Rittenour and I was going to prove it by being the bigger person.

No matter how much I hated her at that moment.

Chapter 8

Aleena

I woke with the headache from hell and a feeling of dread hanging over me.

It could have been from the wine.

It could have been from the fact that I hadn't gone to bed until nearly two a.m., staying up and waiting for Dominic.

It could have been from a million things.

I decided not to think about any of them. Stumbling into workout clothes, I jammed sunglasses onto my face and left the penthouse. It was quiet. Either Dominic was still asleep or he was out doing what I was doing, running off the excesses of a late night, too much food and too much wine.

I'd only recently started running, but I'd grown to like it, appreciating the way it burned calories and revved up my heart. I'd always been too self-conscious to run back home because of my figure. Here, I didn't care. Out on the street, no one looked at me like a freak. It was a great way to clear my head as well. Today, I was trying to pound the headache out of my head with every slap of my feet on the concrete.

I took the route toward the park and spent almost an hour pounding the pavement. By the time I was on my way home, the headache had retreated to almost tolerable levels. So even though my muscles felt like spaghetti, I considered it a win as I rounded the corner that took me back to the penthouse.

I was almost inside when a shadow fell across my path.

I froze.

Joshua stood there.

"Get away from me," I snapped. I really wasn't in the mood.

One of the doormen moved toward us and I held up a hand. I didn't need help. I could deal with this asshole on my own. Dominic wasn't the only one with a mean right hook.

Joshua dipped his head. "Ma'am...I...um." He looked around. "Look, I'm sorry about last night."

"You should be apologizing to Penelope." I crossed my arms over my chest. As much as I disliked her, no woman deserved to be treated like that. No person.

"I did." He looked away again. "Well, I tried anyway." Abruptly, he shoved an envelope at me. "You should see this. You're a nice girl, or you seem like it. You shouldn't be treated like this."

I stared at the envelope and that wicked curl of dread got worse. I felt like a lump had settled in my stomach.

"What..." I stopped and cleared my throat as my voice threatened to crack. "What is this?"

He just continued to hold it out until I had no choice but to take it.

"I'm sorry," he said again. "I was just...I wanted to apologize. To her. And that's when I saw them."

He took off without further explanation, disappearing down the sidewalk at a quick clip.

***

My gut was raw.

Bent over the toilet, I wretched for what felt like the millionth time. I wanted to curl up into a ball and die, but I couldn't do that because I needed to pack my stuff. I needed to get the hell out of here.

But all I could do was sit there.

Slowly, feeling like I'd aged a thousand years in the past few minutes, I forced myself away from the commode and sat with my back against the wall. Staring at nothing, I willed myself to find the energy to move.

I had to move.

I didn't know where Dominic was, but I didn't want to be here, on the floor, stinking of sweat and vomit when he came in.

I didn't want to be surrounded by pictures, by the evidence of how gullible I'd been.

Tears burned my eyes.

I was a *fool*.

I was an idiot.

A naïve, foolish idiot.

And I loved him.

I loved him so much it hurt.

Even now.

If he came in and talked to me, I didn't know

what would happen. Would I let him talk me into staying? Could he talk me into it? I just knew that I lost my head when I was with him. I didn't think clearly, and that's what had made me vulnerable to...I couldn't give him the opportunity to convince me to stay, the chance to humiliate me.

I forced myself upright. Flushing the toilet, I went through the motions of washing my hands, my face. I brushed my teeth and threw the toothbrush away. My mouth still felt nasty so I took a swig of mouthwash. I didn't feel better, but I was back in control of myself. I almost left the pictures on the floor, but in the end, I scooped them up and dumped them on my bed.

I didn't plan on ever sleeping there again.

I didn't know where I was going, or what I would do, but I did know I was leaving here.

Packing would take too long.

I didn't even pack everything, just enough to fill two suitcases. That would get me through a couple of weeks, I knew. I'd learned how to pack light and travel easy, thanks to going back and forth to the Hamptons so often.

The thought of the house and all that had happened there brought a fresh lance of pain through my heart and I wanted to bend over, clutch at my chest, scream from the misery of it. But I didn't.

I just kept packing.

I didn't know how long it had taken, from the time I'd entered the penthouse to when I finally picked up my bag and walked out. I left the keys behind me, a bit of finality, because I didn't plan on coming back. And I didn't need the temptation they would offer. I had to make a clean break.

The doorman was one of the men I didn't know well and still in a dull state of shock, I didn't think to avoid him, just told him I needed a cab. He stared at me, clearly concerned and asked if he could call Dominic.

"No!" I practically shouted the word as panic flooded me.

He held out a hand, almost looking panicked himself. "It's okay, Miss Aleena. I'll get you a cab, of course."

He immediately stepped to the curb and raised his hand. I watched, but didn't really pay attention as a cab pulled up. If I'd been less out of it, I'd have thought something of how long he spoke to the driver before opening the back door for me, but my brain wasn't working at its best, focused only on getting away.

I gave the driver Molly's address as I climbed into the back seat, and once the door was shut, I curled in on myself and cried.

Chapter 9

Dominic

"There's nothing."

The small diner where Kowalski and I sat was bland and nondescript, perfect for this kind of meeting. He'd called me directly since I'd forgotten to give him Aleena's information. He'd agreed that if I was trying to keep this low profile, it was best that I not be seen meeting with a man that any number of people would likely make as a cop.

He wasn't a cop now.

But he had been. And he told me, *once a cop, always a cop.*

I'd had a lot of experience with officers of the law when I'd been a rebellious teenager and I knew that most people could've picked him out of a room as being in law enforcement.

It was the eyes.

They saw everything.

Running my tongue across my teeth, I considered his words, but didn't respond right away.

There could be several ways to take what he'd told me. Either he had nothing to tell me, no updates, or there was nothing he could unearth...if it was that, then I was pissed. He'd said himself that he was the last resort.

I took a sip of my coffee. It was surprisingly good. The diner he'd selected was a hole in the wall, the kind of place I wouldn't have chosen to save my life. Which just meant I didn't always know as much as I like to think I did. The bill had already been put on the table. The coffee cost less than three dollars. I'd paid four times that for coffee that tasted like shit. I made a mental note to make sure I told Aleena about it.

Putting down the cheap, excellent coffee, I tried not to sound accusatory. "What do you mean nothing?"

"Just that." He flipped open the file he'd brought with him. "As of yet, I have nothing to tell you. I've done a surface check with the legit adoption agencies. Now, if your adoption was closed, that makes it more problematic. You have to know the right tricks." He paused and gave me a small, closed-lip smile. "I know the right tricks. I've got some feelers out. There were a few pops, some names that came up, but none of them felt right. A couple of the boys that match your description—blond male, blue eyes—have already come up and I've ID'd them." A shadow flickered through his eyes. "One died before his first birthday. Another passed away from leukemia when he was twelve. Others, I'm working on. We're lucky that only a handful of boys with your description were born in the New York area." He paused and added, "You're sure you were born in New York State?"

"Yes." I nodded. "That's one of the few things my adoptive mother told me."

My phone buzzed. I looked down, checked the number, then set the phone aside. I didn't know it, but if it was important, they'd leave a message.

"I'll continue looking into open adoptions, but I'm going to start checking the closed adoptions, talking to some of the people I know who handled the private ones." Kowalski paused and said, "This will take time."

"I've waited this long." I was frustrated, but not discouraged.

He nodded. "It would help if I could talk to somebody who was there when you were brought home. Any employees, family friends..." He left the sentence hanging.

Grimly, I stared at him and then slowly, I said, "You can try talking to my adopted father, but I doubt he'll be willing to talk at all." I felt half-dead inside as I added, "He barely sees me as his son anymore. He won't go out of his way to help me."

My phone buzzed again. It was the same number. Who the hell kept calling me?

Kowalski glanced at it. "If it's urgent, I'm fine to wait."

I shook my head. "This takes priority."

"Of course." He reached into his jacket and withdrew a pen and paper. "Your father's information?"

I had to flip through my phone to find it and a text came through at the same time.

This is Geoffrey Carter from Regent. I apologize for disturbing you, but we keep your number on hand in cases of urgent matters and I need to speak with you regarding Aleena Davison. Please call me at your earliest convenience.

I stared at the message, my stomach twisting in dread.

I stared so long, I completely forgot Kowalski was there until he cleared his throat. "Is everything okay?"

No, I wanted to say. Instead, I lied. "Ah, yeah." I cleared my throat and tried again. "Yeah."

Rattling off the information he needed, I glanced around and rose. Tossing a few bills on the table, I looked at him. "Is that all?"

"For now. I'll be—"

The jangling of the bell over the door cut off the rest of his sentence. I started to walk as I punched in the number that had appeared in my history.

"This is Snow."

"Mr. Snow, Geoffrey Carter. I'm sorry to bother you, but Aleena Davison just left here. She had suitcases with her."

"Suit...what the fuck are you talking about?" I dimly realized I was shouting into the phone and people were staring. I didn't even care.

"She was upset..."

I didn't bother to listen to the rest. I jogged

116

toward my car at the end of the street. Maxwell saw me coming and hurried around to open the door, but I waved him away. "Back to the penthouse. *Now*."

* * *

"She'd left to go running,"

Geoffrey told me. His face was pale and if I hadn't been so angry and upset, I might've felt bad for him.

"When she came back, she seemed fine at that point, maybe a little tired. But then a man approached her."

"Who?" I crossed my arms over my chest, mostly to keep from grabbing the doorman and shaking him. That wouldn't get answers any faster

Geoffrey held out a couple pictures. "I had security print these from our cameras. He gave her something. I believe that's what upset her."

I grabbed the pictures and found myself staring at the downward angle of Joshua's face.

Joshua, the prick I'd kicked out of my apartment last night. I was going to kill him if he was the reason she'd left.

The images showed him passing over an envelope to her.

"Did she open it out here? Did you see what was inside?"

"No," Geoffrey said, his voice quiet. "I'm sorry."

I just shook my head and headed inside.

The elevator moved too slow. If I could've run to the top, I would have, but that was too many stairs to climb, especially at a fast pace. I was impatient though, desperate to get upstairs. I had to see what had chased her out. There was something.

Something.

There had to be.

She wouldn't have just left for no reason.

I found the note I'd left her by the phone and there was no sign she'd even seen it. Usually, if she saw a note, she left a response. A smiley face, an *ok*...something. This simple note—*Gone to see PI*—was just my black chicken scratch on white paper. Oddly forlorn.

I moved through each room. Living room. Kitchen. Hallway. Up the stairs to the bathroom. The sour, acrid stink of somebody getting sick lingered beneath the mint of mouthwash and toothpaste.

My own stomach roiled in sympathy.

I moved onto her bedroom and the pieces immediately clicked into place.

Numb, I dropped down onto her bed and picked up the pictures.

I found myself thinking of last night and how Penelope had turned into a living, breathing vine, twining herself around me until I'd had to forcibly remove her.

Her mouth had been too cool under mine, her lips too thin. Too not...still, she'd clung to me and each attempt I'd made to make her stop had only made her cling tighter. It had been like being

118

suffocated and for a few bleak, black minutes, I'd flashed back to the year I'd spent in the dark.

The world had realigned itself when she slid her tongue along my lips and said, "I can give you *so much more* than she can..."

I'd stopped trying to be gentle at that point and had shoved her away from me, staring at her in disgust. "You can't give me what you don't have, Penelope."

She'd said nothing else, just watched me with a triumphant expression on her face. That look made sense now.

She'd set this up.

Both of them had.

And now Aleena thought...

I shot upright.

Geoffrey. He'd said he knew where she was going.

***

"I can't make her talk to you, Dominic."

Molly glanced at me and then back over her shoulder. Some short, squat woman with a stern face and square jaw was glancing at us. A new boss? I don't know. Didn't care.

She sighed, "Look, she's pretty..."

I dumped the pictures down on the table and Molly's gaze flicked to them. Judging by the expression on her face, Aleena had told her about

119

them. Not surprising. What I was surprised about, however, was that Molly hadn't punched me when I'd walked in. I had the feeling that if I'd shown up at Molly's apartment, I might not have been so lucky.

"Penelope set it up," I said bluntly. "I think she set it all up, including when Joshua decided to get too hands-on, too pushy, making me get involved. I think Joshua acted like he was so drunk, he could barely move. Otherwise, how, not even an hour later, was he sober enough to go to her place and apologize? Clear-headed enough to see us and take pictures? *Then* get digital stills from the pictures? And he waited until this morning to show her?"

Molly's mouth went tight as she pushed through each picture, but she shook her head. "Even if I believe you, I can't make her talk to you."

"Try."

Her eyes moved from the pictures to me, and they softened.

She believed me.

"I can try. But that's it."

Chapter 10

Aleena

"A fancy dinner out isn't my idea of a pep-talk." Grimacing, I looked down at the sweatshirt I'd pulled on to combat the cool drizzle that had settled over the city this evening. I rather liked it. It matched my mood. I gave Molly a baleful look, although the fact that my eyes were red-rimmed and my clothes looked like something from a thrift store probably made me look less than threatening.

"Oh, this isn't a pep-talk." She gave me a cheerful look that made me want to drown her in the nearest puddle. Cheerfully.

"Then what is it?" I reached for the cranberry vodka I'd ordered. If I couldn't drown myself in brownie batter ice cream, I was going with the next best alternative. Booze.

"An intervention." She reached for her martini and settled back in the seat with a happy sigh.

Unlike me, Molly was totally dressed for this place, wearing a cute sea green dress that matched her eyes, her bright hair swept up into a crazy topknot that left loose tendrils falling down all around her face. She looked flirty and fun and adorably sexy.

I looked like a slob and that just made me more depressed. "I don't want an intervention."

I wanted Dominic. And I hated myself for it.

The smile on her face widened. "Oh, relax. You'll

121

feel better when it's done."

"No. I won't." I went to take another sip of my drink, but the drink didn't make it halfway to my lips.

A familiar laugh drifted toward my ears and I froze, everything in me going cold.

That laugh.

Slowly, I put the glass back down. Better to do it now before I got up and found Penelope Rittenour, grabbed the elegant coif of her hair and slammed her pretty, perfect face into the nearest flat surface.

I was going to get over this.

I was going to get over him.

I was going to do it without killing either of them.

Elegant greenery provided the suggestion of privacy, although it wasn't truly private. All I had to do was try, and I'd be able to see through the leaves and lattice work. Granted, I would look like an idiot. Still. I could see...I shook my head.

Carefully, I pulled the napkin from my lap and reached for my purse. "I don't want to be here." I made a move to stand up and Molly reached out and caught my arm.

"Sit." She glared at me. Her fingers squeezed my arm with enough force to catch my attention and she didn't let go.

"Hey!" I snapped. Jerking against her grip, I tried to twist away.

Molly was small, petite, bordering on delicate. I shouldn't have had that much trouble breaking free from her grip.

The key word being *shouldn't*.

She was a hell of a lot stronger than she looked.

"Sit." When I narrowed my eyes at her, she stuck out her tongue at me. Then, with an arched eyebrow, she tilted her head to one side and said quietly, "You love the guy."

It was pointless to deny it. "Well, I'm going to do whatever I can to change that." Yeah, I loved him. I loved him so much it was choking me, killing me, squeezing the air out of my lungs. It was a gaping wound inside me now and nothing would ever fill it.

"Yeah. Good luck with that." Her eyes softened and she shook her head. "Aleena, I've been in love. Maybe not the big *L*, which I think is what you've got going on. But even those little *l* break-ups hurt like...well, hell. It's not as easy as that to just get over it. And if he's the real thing, you'll never get over him." She paused and then added, "Besides, what happened... it's not what you think."

I would have laughed if I'd had the air to do it, but the pain was suffocating me, like a hand around my throat.. More than once since I'd seen those pictures, I'd found myself on the verge of passing out because I couldn't breathe.

"Just how am I supposed to misinterpret what I saw? They were fucking pictures, Molly, not exactly open to interpretation." I fought to keep my voice low. The last thing I needed was the humiliation of him finding me here. Of them *both* finding me here. Seeing me, especially dressed like this. It was like my worst nightmare come true.

"You're wrong," she said. "It was a setup. All of

123

it. Now listen."

She pressed a finger to her lips and it was as if the entire place had gotten the message. All but Penelope and her voice carried. Even the music was quieter. Noticeably so.

Molly placed her phone on the table in front of us and I watched as she tugged out a pair of ear buds, sliding the jack into place. She fiddled a moment and muttered, "This is so cloak and dagger. I love it."

"What—?"

"Shh!" She pressed a finger to her lips again and then lifted up an ear bud.

I stared at it and she shoved it closer. There was no point in arguing with her. Sighing, I tucked it into my ear while she did the same with the one she held. A moment later, two familiar voices filled my ear. They were loud, clear and unmistakable.

Penelope's voice grated on me and Dominic's low murmur made me want to cry. Or hit something. My hands curled into tight little balls, nails biting into my palms. The word *catfight* had never sounded so appealing as it did then. I wanted to go over and scratch her eyes out. I wanted to sink my hands in her hair and yank. I wanted to be as unladylike as possible and I wanted to hurt her. Hurt him, too. Hurt him like he'd hurt me.

"Dominic, I must say, I was surprised to hear from you." She spoke in that low, almost raspy way I suspected she thought was appealing. It wasn't, at least not to me, but then again, I wasn't really her target audience. For all I knew, Dominic thought it was damn sexy. For all I knew, Dominic thought *she* was damn sexy.

He does, a snide voice inside my head sneered. *You saw photographic evidence, remember?*

"Surprised?" Dominic said.

My heart lurched at the sound of his voice and I curled my hands around the cushioned seat under me. It was better than hurting myself. I was hurting enough as it was.

"But of course." Penelope's voice lowered. "You know I'm seeing Joshua now. It's too late for us, Dominic."

Frowning, I shot Molly a glance. What was Penelope playing at? Molly shook her head and jabbed a finger at the phone, wordlessly telling me to keep listening.

I rolled my eyes and then turned to glare at the screen of greenery and latticework that blocked them from view. They were maybe ten feet away. Too close for me to really hear them without the help of Molly's electronic eavesdropping. I was torn between wanting to see them and not wanting to. Both options made me feel sick to my stomach.

"Joshua..." Dominic's laugh was humorless. "Yes, I think the both of you proved how serious you two are."

"About last night, Joshua was drunk," Penelope said. "He's a good man. He didn't mean anything. He—"

"I talked to him a couple hours ago. He told me everything. Including the ten thousand dollar debt you covered for him if he went along with your little scheme."

I jerked and if Molly hadn't caught my drink, it would have splattered across the fine white tablecloth. My heart started to gallop in my chest.

"I...Dominic." She sounded brittle now. Less confident. Strained even. "I don't know what you're talking about."

"It wasn't that hard to find out. I know all about Joshua's gambling debts. His family's cut him off. He's expected to man up, get a job, deal with it on his own." Dominic sounded amused. "Apparently, his idea of manning up is pretending to get drunk and rough up women, then taking pictures of them and passing them around. Interesting occupation. Is he an actor? A reverse private investigator? He did a bang-up job, I've got to say."

The silence that followed was so complete, I could hear breathing coming through the ear buds. I squirmed around and shoved at the greenery. I didn't care if I looked like an idiot now. I had to see them. I had to know if it was for real.

Dominic was staring at Penelope, but his expression was anything but friendly. Penelope sat facing opposite him and I could see most of her face, the rigid line of her shoulders and spine. She reached for her wine glass and sipped, lowered it. Sipped again. Lowered it.

Finally, she spoke and her voice was smooth, but with a ragged edge underneath. "Really, Dominic, that's quite an interesting fantasy you've concocted."

"Come off it, Penelope." Dominic leaned forward and gave her a cold, deadly smile. It was the smile

I'd seen him give a dozen people in the boardroom and it was the kind of smile that made wise people back down. "Joshua was smart. He knew that I could do a lot of damage so when I made him a deal, he realized it was better to just accept. Do you really want to fuck with me on this?"

Her laugh came through the phone bright and happy. "Are you threatening me, Dominic? What are you planning to do? Hit me?"

"Actually, yes."

Ice grabbed me, but only for a moment. I started to get up, but again, Molly stopped me. "Wait," she said, her voice low.

"I'll hit you right where it hurts, Penelope."

I heard the sound of paper shuffling and turned my head, once more staring through the small gap I'd created.

"It's interesting, the things men will tell you when you hold a great deal of leverage over them." Dominic smiled and flipped a piece of paper around for her to see.

I couldn't see it, but I knew it was a picture, a large one. Penelope glanced at it. "That's hardly anything for me to be concerned about, Dominic. You and I kissed. It's nothing shocking."

"This wasn't us kissing." Dominic leaned forward and said quietly. "This was you throwing yourself at me for the two seconds it took me to get you off."

Even from where I sat, I could see her stiffening. She relaxed almost immediately though and plucked up another piece of paper—another picture—and gave it a disinterested look. Her smile was cool as she said, "This lasted a lot longer than two seconds."

Dominic smirked at her. "That's because you wouldn't take no for an answer and you kept pushing." He looked as though he was considering something and then he said softly, "I never had any desire to kiss you, or do anything else with you, and you should be grateful, Penelope. If I had, you would have run away screaming." His voice darkened. "You couldn't handle me."

"Oh, let me guess," she said, leaning forward and giving a mock shudder. "You are too tormented, too twisted by your tragic childhood. Am I too much a lady for your twisted needs?"

"I'd never mistake you for a lady, Penelope." Dominic gave her a devilish smile. "What you are is not enough of a woman to satisfy me."

Her mouth tightened.

"What would you do if I wanted to tie you to the bed and whip you until your ass was cherry red?"

She'd picked up her wineglass after his insult and it made a faintly musical sound when she dropped it, breaking into tiny little shards.

She didn't seem to notice, just sat staring at him in dull shock.

Then she swallowed. "That's not amusing, Dominic. Really. I can see that you're upset, but there's no need—"

"I'm not joking." His eyes were hard, bright, but without warmth. "There are a dozen rumors floating around about me and my sexual proclivities. People either feed them or they ignore them. Clearly, you

128

fall into the same camp as my mother. You ignore them."

"That's..."

A server appeared at their side, but Dominic waved him away. "You can deal with the glass in a moment," he said, his voice harsh.

"But, Mr. Snow."

"In a moment," Dominic snapped.

Penelope was now looking everywhere but at Dominic.

"You look upset," Dominic said, his voice silky. He leaned forward and Penelope shrank back.

Both of us saw it.

Dominic looked amused by it.

I wanted to smack her.

She finds out he likes kinky sex and that makes him dirty?

"Why are you trying to fuck with me, Penelope? Is it because I didn't want *you*...or is it because I wanted someone better. Because I wanted Aleena?"

Her gaze jerked back to his and she seemed to come out of her dazed state, her spine stiffening. A second later, he had water dripping down his face.

Seething, Penelope put her water glass back on the table and rose. "Her." Scorn dripped from her voice like the droplets of water from Dominic's face. "You could have had *me*—and please note, the word is *had*. You could have had me. Do you know how many men would've killed to be in your position? And yet you chose that common whore."

I slid from the booth. This time, Molly made no attempt to stop me.

Penelope turned and started to walk away, but stopped when she saw me. She tried to smile, but it wobbled, then fell away as I stepped toward her. It struck me then that the restaurant was empty. It was only us and the staff.

Dominic had set this up.

Him and Molly.

I glanced past Penelope to see him standing there, watching me, emotion burning hot in his eyes.

Swallowing hard, I looked back at Penelope. Her gaze flitted around, bouncing off everything but me. She couldn't even look at me.

My anger dissipated into something else. "What kind of miserable, unhappy person must you be that you constantly go out of your way to make other people as miserable and unhappy as you are?" I asked. She started to pass me, but I moved, cutting her off. "Don't."

Penelope drew back her head, her nostrils flaring. "Move out of my way."

"Answer my question," I shot back. "Why do you do this? Are you so miserable that this is the only way you can exist? By making everybody else unhappy too?"

"Miserable?" Her laugh was shrill. She pressed a hand to her chest as she looked around, as though expecting somebody else to voice their shock as well, but there was nobody, save for Dominic and Molly. "I'm one of the richest women in the entire state. The mayor, the governor, *celebrities* call me out of the blue to ask me to attend their functions. I'm *Penelope Rittenour* and I'm—"

130

"Miserable." I interrupted. "Knowing people, having money...none of that makes you happy. Do you even remember the last time you were happy? Have you ever been happy?"

Her mouth fell open.

I walked around her and went to Dominic. Halfway there, I paused and looked back at her. She was still standing there, staring.

"I feel sorry for you," I said quietly.

Then I turned my head and looked back at Dominic. Just a few feet separated us now and it felt like miles.

I forced myself to take the first step, then the next. His gaze rested on my face and I felt like I could hardly bear it.

Finally, I was just a few inches away and the pounding of my heart was so loud, I wondered if he could hear it. I felt naked under his gaze. Desperate for respite, I looked away and my gaze fell on the mirrors on the opposite wall.

Again, it struck me how out of place I was. It wasn't just because I wasn't dressed for this place. It went much deeper than that and I knew it.

"I'm sorry." My voice was barely a whisper. "I'm so sorry."

Dominic held out his hand without a word.

Slowly, I took it and the tightness around my lungs eased. For the first time since I'd seen those pictures, I could breathe again.

Chapter 11

Dominic

One thing I had come to love about Aleena was that silence with her had been easy. With her, I never felt out of place in the quiet. I never felt like I had to say something when I wanted to say nothing at all.

But now, the silence was different.

I didn't feel moved to say anything, but I had the feeling she did. She sat next to me on seats of luxurious leather as we sped through the night and I could feel the words trembling on her tongue.

Yet she held them back.

I didn't prompt her to speak. I didn't see the point. I knew how miserable it was to have things inside of you that you wanted to say but couldn't manage to give voice to. I also knew how terrible it was to want silence and have people pushing you to speak. If she wanted silence, she could be silent. If she wanted to speak or felt she had to, then she would have to find her own way to figure out what she wanted to say.

Just then, I was dealing with enough turmoil of my own.

I was dealing with enough *emotion* on my own.

I hurt and I didn't like it. That was actually putting it mildly. It fucking pissed me off. I was furious. Furious at her, at myself, at Penelope. She'd told Penelope she felt sorry for her and even that infuriated me. Penelope didn't deserve her pity or her sympathy.

Where had Aleena's sympathy or her kind thoughts been when she'd looked at those pictures and just believed. Believed the worst of me.

What would you have done? The rational part of me tried to gain control, but I didn't want to be rational.

Fury all but consumed me, burning through every single part of me and there was nothing I could do about it. Finally, the car rumbled to a stop in front of the penthouse and I climbed out, closing my eyes and taking a deep breath. For a long moment, I simply stood, and then I turned and held out a hand to Aleena.

She accepted and we started toward the building.

Need already had my muscles knotted and I could see the two of us. Could see the things I wanted to do, the things I would do...

And halfway to the door, I stopped.

Aleena looked up at me, apprehension on her face. I hated that look, but I couldn't do anything about it.

I gave her my keys. Actually, they were her keys.

She had left them behind when she left me. I'd taken them with me tonight, intending to give them back.

"Do you still want these?" It was a struggle to keep my voice level.

"Yes," she said, her voice soft. "Dominic, I'm sorry. I—"

I shook my head. "Go on up. I'll be back later."

"Where you going?" she asked. Her voice broke as her head fell.

It was like she'd punched me straight in the heart. I made a move as if to touch her, but I stopped. If I touched her now, it was all done. If I touched her now, I would do things I didn't think she was ready for and I would ruin what we had. It was tenuous at the moment as it was.

"I can't be around you right now." My voice was as harsh as hers was hesitant and I felt as much as saw her stiffen. "I'm going to go to the club. Or to work. Something. I don't know. But I need to...I need some time before I can be around you. I'm sorry."

She flinched when I mentioned the club and by the time I was done speaking, her face had crumpled and tears had filled her eyes. "I'm sorry," she whispered again.

"I know." I jerked my head in a nod. "We'll...talk. Later. But for now..."

I went to turn away, but she caught my arm. "Please don't leave."

"I can't stay here." I stared at her hand, her slim fingers, warm and gold, soft and slim, on my arm. My stomach twisted, knotted. "I can't be around you.

I need..."

"I know what you need." The words were ragged, as if torn from her. "I...Dominic, I need it too. Please don't leave me right now. I'm sorry. Please."

She moved closer, so close I could smell her. Smell her skin, her hair. So close, I could feel the heat of her. Impossibly, my body tensed even more. I wanted to shake off her hand, but I couldn't move.

"You don't know what you're asking for."

Her words were soft, but sincere. "Then show me."

Control had become a brittle thing and when she touched my cheek, I knew it was about to break. I caught her wrist, squeezed lightly, felt the delicate bones beneath my fingers. "Be sure, Aleena."

"I am."

I took a step back and inhaled slowly. I still needed some control. When I was ready, I held out my hand and waited for her to take that final step.

Her hand slid into mine without any hesitation.

My blood started to pump hot and thick, while the savage need that had been building inside me rose to a deafening roar.

Chapter 12

Aleena

Be sure, he'd told me.

I couldn't say he hadn't warned me.

I was now as helpless as I'd ever been. Still, I was resolved to see it through. I'd hurt him, letting my own insecurity override everything else. I wasn't going to let him go to someone else for what he needed, even if it was only to watch. Besides, I needed this too.

I held a scarf clutched in my hands, because I couldn't speak. Dominic had gagged me, and not with a cloth or anything like that. No, he'd used a ball gag for the first time and my jaw ached.

He'd spent nearly twenty minutes restraining me, but there was nothing ornate about the restraints. I knew why. He'd used the time to calm himself, center himself, and to draw it out. Now, face down and my cheek pressed to the floor, I closed my eyes and waited.

I'd been waiting several minutes, the

anticipation killing me, but still better than the emptiness I'd felt without him.

Something flicked between my thighs, not touching, but the promise of more.

I twitched and instinctively tried to draw them together, but the spreader bar made it impossible.

I couldn't even move away or roll to my side, because my ankles weren't the only thing restrained. He'd brought out another bar, this one attaching to my collar. It had loops on the end for my wrists, loops that could slide with the flick of a latch.

I was kneeling face down with my ass in the air and my hands near my face, locked in place, a scarf in one hand. If it got to be too much, I was to drop that scarf. That was my alternative for a safe word.

Lashes flicked between my thighs and the sound of my muffled moan rose to my ears. I was ready, needy. I didn't just need him though, I needed his forgiveness, needed to prove myself, and this was the way to do it.

I felt something against my back.

"You didn't trust me." Dominic's voice was soft, emotionless. Yet I heard the pain in it. I'd seen it in his eyes. I could have begged him to forgive me if I would, but I wouldn't. What I would do was let him have what he needed from me. Let him give me what I needed from him.

He brought the flogger down, and I gasped when the lashes spread out over my ass and between my thighs. It wasn't the leather and fur one, and it confirmed what I'd already known. This was going to hurt.

138

The flogger struck my ass again, sending heat coursing through me.

"I'm not pleased about it, Aleena. Do you understand?" Something in his tone shifted, and I could hear the man beneath the Dom. "This doesn't work if you don't trust me."

I nodded the best I could, feeling the soft velvet rub against my neck.

"You're going to be punished for it now."

I nodded again.

"Do you want to be punished?"

Another nod. It was the truth. I wanted this, wanted the pain he could give me and the release that came with it. Release for me, and for him.

He struck me again, harder this time, and I screamed against the ball gag. It was the harshest edge of pleasure and the sweetest slice of pain. I let my head fall forward, my eyes closing as I absorbed the next few blows.

Sweat dripped from me when he stopped and came to kneel behind me. My ass burned, my breath coming in harsh pants. His hand tangled in my hair and he yanked me up.

"You won't ever doubt me like that again, will you?"

I would have shaken my head, but I couldn't, not with him holding my hair so tight.

Then it wasn't necessary because he was freeing me from the ball-gag. "No." It was a whimper and a plea and a promise. My voice was hoarse.

"Good." He slid a hand down my stomach and pressed me back against him. Oh, fuck. He was

139

naked.

He plunged two fingers into my pussy and I nearly screamed. I was wet, but not stretched and he wasn't being gentle. His fingers pumped in and out, twisting and rubbing against my walls.

"I thought about making you go all night without a climax, but I decided that wasn't what either of us needed."

He pressed his thumb against my clit and I moaned.

"No words unless I ask a question, but you can make all the noises you want."

I rolled my hips and rode his hand. He made no move to stop me. Instead, he moved with me and I felt his cock, hot against my ass.

"In fact, I want you to scream." He pushed a third finger inside me. "Scream for me, baby."

His fingers twisted again and that was it. I shuddered, my hips bucking against his hand as I came. His other hand pinched my nipple, rolling and pulling until the whining sound turned into a loud cry. Not quite a scream, but close.

"You see, I need to mark you, make you understand—you're mine. I'm yours." He spoke against my ear as he continued to pump his fingers in and out, harsh and fast, working me higher and higher. "Do you understand me, baby?"

"Yes, sir." The words were little more than air.

"Good."

He stopped abruptly, I moaned, trembling, so close to coming again.

"I'm taking your ass tonight, Aleena."

I sucked in a breath.

"Not a single word unless it's the answer to a question, or the ball-gag goes back in."

He pushed me forward, his grip on my hair guiding me back to the floor. I was helpless, unable to brace myself. He controlled me, made sure I was flat and steady and then I gasped as I felt his thumbs on the cheeks of my ass, pulling me wide.

"If I didn't want to hear you scream for me, I'd have it back in."

I felt the cool liquid trickle down my ass, then gasped as his thumb pushed inside me. His finger followed, working my ass open for what was to come.

He spoke as he pressed a second finger forward, his voice blunt and direct. "It's going to hurt you some. You have to take it because I can't make it not hurt. If it's too much, you remember your safe word, right?"

I nodded, apprehension grabbing and twisting me. The burn from his fingers was fading into pleasure, but I knew he was so much bigger than his fingers.

"I'm also going to mark you tonight," he promised. "And you won't cover it up." His free hand reached down and grasped my collar. He didn't pull on it, but I could feel his fingers caressing the soft material. "You're mine, and by the time we're done, you're going to know exactly what that means."

He pulled his fingers out so suddenly that I gasped. And then I felt it, the blunt head of his cock pressing against my asshole. I tried to relax, but my body was coiled too tight. He pushed forward slowly and I sucked in a desperate breath through my nostrils, trying to adjust the head of his cock as it squeezed in past the ring of muscle. He held there for a moment, rocking slowly. He wasn't moving much, just shallow sways of his body that fooled my body into relaxing. The second I did, he slid deeper. I tensed.

He fisted a hand in my hair and jerked.

Gasping, I arched up. So focused on that pain, I forgot to fight the invasion of my body and he worked deeper, then deeper.

Pain bloomed, threatening to overtake me and he slowed, shifting to those slow, shallow thrusts and lulling me into relaxing again.

I shuddered around him as he smoothed a hand down the curve of my hip, along my butt and then administered a series of quick hard slaps that left my skin stinging and my clit throbbing, desperate for release. As though I'd told him that, he slid his other hand around and stroked me.

I climaxed almost immediately, quick and hard.

And he drove completely inside, in one ruthless thrust.

I screamed, the pain brutal, overshadowing the pleasure of my orgasm. I twitched and twisted, tried to tear away from him. He pulled my hair and forced me up, forced my body to accommodate him, accept him. His teeth scraped against the side of my neck.

"Is it too much?" he asked.

"No," I said, not sure if he believed me.

He rotated his hips. "Say the word. Tell me..."

The word.

The safe word.

It formed in my mind. On my lips.

He rotated his hips again and slapped the flat of his hand against my mound, directly against my clit. I felt him swell inside my ass, impossibly and painfully large, and he said again, "Say the word if you want me to stop."

Suddenly, I remembered the look on his face when I'd seen him in the restaurant. I thought of the pain he must have been in when he'd realized I'd left without even asking him to explain. I'd thought he'd broken my heart, but I'd been the one who'd done wrong. I'd violated the trust between us. I needed to prove that I trusted him.

This was how.

"No." I twisted my head around and kissed him, ignoring the pain. No. I welcomed it and rolled my hips, riding his cock. I screamed against his mouth as the movement stretched me wider. I bit down on his bottom lip and he cupped my breasts, squeezing in a way I would've found painful if he hadn't been buried, balls deep, in my ass.

He broke the kiss and twisted my head back around so that he could have access to my neck. As his mouth latched on to a spot just above my collar, I knew he was making good on his promise to mark me. He gripped my hip and my hair and held me steady as he plunged inside, over and over, his thrusts pushing me off my knees.

I didn't know when the pain slid away into pleasure, but it did and I found myself driving back onto him and begging, pleading. The hand that steadied my hip moved between my thighs, plunging in and out as he flicked his thumb against my clitoris. He pulsed inside me, swelled, and I knew he was close.

His thumb circled and teased at my clit and then he bit down as he shoved himself deep inside me. Hard.

I came only a moment before he did and as I heard him say my name, blackness danced before me.

***

He must have taken off all of restraints while I was passed out because when I came to, he was carrying me into the shower.

He cleaned me, washing me from head to toe, including my hair and I didn't even protest when he used the wrong shampoo. I didn't exactly mind the idea of smelling like him. Besides, I barely had the energy to stand there as it was.

The water stung against every spot the flogger had landed and I could feel the place on my neck where he'd bitten me. I ached all over and when he used a soft wash cloth and rubbed me between the cheeks of my ass, I whimpered.

"Shhh," he murmured.

Ducking my head, I closed my eyes and pretended I wasn't blushing over the shocking intimacy of it. I felt his lips press against the space between my shoulder blades and shivered at the gentle touch, such a stark contrast to what we'd just done.

I was about ready to fall asleep on my feet when he turned off the water and then, again, picked me up.

"I can walk," I mumbled, my head falling against his chest.

"And I can carry you," he said against my hair.

When he lay me down, at first, I didn't notice anything odd.

Then, I realized that the bed didn't feel quite right. My eyes flew open and I looked around. The steel gray walls surrounding me weren't my walls. The maroon accents weren't mine.

"Dominic?"

He curled up in the bed next to me and drew me into the curve of his body. "You stay with me tonight," he said, his voice flat.

His fingers brushed against the spot on my neck where he'd marked me. His voice softened. "Will you stay with me?"

Mute, I nodded. All of the emotions that had been just below the surface came bubbling up. Eyes blurring with tears, I turned into him and wrapped my arms around his waist. "I'm so sorry."

His hand curved over the back of my neck. "Next time, trust in me," he said, his voice ragged.

"I will," I promised as I felt the tears trailing down my cheek.

He held me tighter until I fell asleep.

145

Chapter 13

Dominic

Three days had passed since she'd cried herself to sleep in my arms Saturday night.

Sunday, when she'd tried to talk about it, I'd simply asked if she trusted me.

"Yes." Then she'd looked away, but I'd still seen the shine of tears in her eyes. "I should have trusted you more. I was wrong. Can you—"

I'd kissed her to cut the words off and said, "It's over. We don't look back. You trust me. I trust you."

We hadn't spoken of it since and as far as I was concerned, it was done.

What I was finding disconcerting was that I found myself thinking of words like...*love.* She'd said them to me, so easily. Only once, but I knew she'd meant them. I hadn't been able to say them to her out loud, but lately, more and more, I found myself saying them silently, in my head.

Last night, I'd even mouthed them against her shoulder as she fell asleep. In my bed. Again.

I'd thought about telling her.

Maybe I would. Tonight. I smiled at the thought of it. Maybe...

"Mr. Snow."

I came to a halt as Stan Kowalski rose from the bench just outside the front doors of *Trouver L'Amour.* Annette had suggested benches scattered around the grounds for those who'd like to walk around and talk in a more structured and protected environment.

I hadn't foreseen having a private investigator use one of them to lie in wait for me, but clearly, that was what he'd been doing.

"Good morning, Mr. Kowalski," I said slowly. I forced myself to push aside all the thoughts of Aleena and focus on him. He was here for a reason.

He smiled at me. Tapping an envelope against his thigh, he strode toward me. "Oh, it's a beautiful morning, that's for sure." He stopped a few feet away and nodded. "Yes, very beautiful."

I eyed him thoughtfully, then asked, "Have you learned anything new?"

"Yes." He nodded, satisfaction evident in his voice. "Oh, yes, I have, Mr. Snow. I think I've got something that could well help us find your birth mother."

Serving HIM continues in the final installment Vol. 6, release June 19th. Don't miss the steamy conclusion to Aleena and Dominic's story.

Acknowledgement

First, we would like to thank all of our readers. Without you, our books would not exist. We truly appreciate each and every one of you.

A big "thanks" goes out to all the Facebook fans, street team, beta readers, and advanced reviewers. You are a HUGE part of the success of the series.

We have to thank our PA, Shannon Hunt. Without you our lives would be a complete and utter mess. Also a big thank you goes out to our editor Lynette and our wonderful cover designer, Sinisa. You make our ideas and writing look so good.

About The Authors

MS Parker

M. S. Parker is a USA Today Bestselling author and the author of the Erotic Romance series, Club Privè and Chasing Perfection.

Living in Southern California, she enjoys sitting by the pool with her laptop writing on her next spicy romance.

Growing up all she wanted to be was a dancer, actor or author. So far only the latter has come true but M. S. Parker hasn't retired her dancing shoes just yet. She is still waiting for the call for her to appear on Dancing With The Stars.

When M. S. isn't writing, she can usually be found reading– oops, scratch that! She is always writing.

Cassie Wild

Cassie Wild loves romance. Every since she was eight years old she's been reading every romance novel she could get her hands on, always dreaming of writing her own romance novels.

When MS Parker approached her about co-authoring the Serving HIM series, it didn't take Cassie many seconds to say a big yes!!

Serving HIM is only the beginning to the collaboration between MS Parker and Cassie Wild. Another series is already in the planning stages.

Made in the USA
Las Vegas, NV
11 October 2021

31861563R00089